THE WHISTLER

Nikhil Nannaware

RG books

Published By

Redgrab Books Pvt. Ltd.

942, Mutthiganj, Prayagraj, 211003

www.redgrabbooks.com

contact@redgrabbooks.com

Price in india :200/- INR

First published by Redgrab Books in 2022

Copyright © 2022 Redgrab Books Pvt. Ltd.

Copyright Text © 2022 Nikhil Nannaware

Printed and bound in India

Cover Design & Typesetting by Redgrab Books team

ISBN : 978-93-95697-00-2

The author asserts the moral right to be identified as the author of this work

Dedication

To all those,
Who trusted me, thanks!
Dear reader, you are also one of them!

Prologue

There is an old saying that every story has two sides. Say the happier and the tragic one, the brighter and the darkest one. Maybe, the wrong one and the right one. But the catch is that the coin has three sides.

There are too many stories around, and multiple versions of the same story as the characters. The same tale, if narrated from a different perspective, you'll be surprised to know the facts. The facts you might knew about but didn't believe could give you heartache or make you feel like the happiest person ever. The facts you might have lived but don't remember, rather, don't want to remember; or the facts, that you want to live, but maybe you can't. And what makes things interesting is another fact, when the story ends where it has begun!

It was the first day of the New Year. After dusk, neither in shiny nor the darkest hour of the day, somewhere in the south of the city of Vizag, one of the three wagons had some noise on the abandoned railway tracks. A red light was glowing in the last wagon from where the noise was coming out. People were screaming out of their lives as if someone was killing them; turns out that someone actually was killing them!

After around twenty minutes, there were two gunshots; and another two after fifteen minutes. A few leaves flew by the wind in between and made a creaking noise after getting crushed as the young man of twenty-five walked through it. He was 5.8 feet tall with a lean body and a handsome face.

Under a cream-colored glass frame, he had completely black eyes with stern expressions and zero emotions. His lips curled into a smile while he walked carelessly, putting his hands to his back. A gush of wind came through, and his long silky hair over his forehead flew slightly. He seemed satisfied with the scene before him - there lay two corps in the bloodbath, and everything was red. His blue shirt was soaked in blood, and he seemed to enjoy the cold-blooded massacre he did.

He climbed down the wagon calmly, blowing a whistle.

CONTENTS

The Dead End

Her subordinate provided the information as she reached near the wagons on the track. "Detective, these two are local goons of the area, both dead because of the bullets. Not sure which bullet killed them first. Maybe post-mortem report could tell that."

"What does that mean?" The detective asked.

"They have two bullets, one in the heart and the other one between the eyes." The subordinate replied.

Kirti looked at her subordinate and seemed to have some thoughts. In between, she walked to the corps and noticed the wounds on their bodies. 'Something's terrible in the way', she thought. "Before someone shot them, they were severally beaten. Looks like beaten till internal organs were damaged," she said.

"How come you sure about the internal organs damage, detective?"

"Their mouths are bloody way much more than usual. This happens mostly because of the internal damage." She said without looking at her subordinate while trying to observe something more out of it if she could. They spent some more time inspecting the site and returned to the police station, leaving two constables at the site.

After two days, in the police station, the subordinate sat in the chair, and Kirti stood, taking the support of the table while bending her left leg.

"Who would kill someone like this?" The subordinate asked.

"According to the postmortem report, they were killed

by the bullets in their hearts. Another one was just to make sure they were dead. Both have broken ribs and bones. This is someone who hated them to death." She speculated. "If it were just a killing, whoever he is, would have them just with the bullets, but they were tortured before getting killed. Looks like the bastard celebrated New Year with the red color on 1st January!" She took a pause. "What do we have on the victims?"

"Ma'am, they were just ordinary goons in the area who would beat someone for the money. None of them has killed anyone yet—their last whereabouts are quite interesting, though. Three days ago they robbed someone but were caught by the police. Someone made their bail. But the one who was robbed, we don't have anything on him."

"Who made their bail?"

"That..." the subordinate was silent.

Kirti glared at him, and he narrated the story. "Ma'am, someone named Mr. Sinha did the bail. But we couldn't find anything about him. The details are bogus, leading us to nowhere."

"So, that makes the one they robbed important to us, I guess." Kirti nodded like she figured out something and kept her calm.

As for the subordinate, he could not find anything about the one who was robbed. The advocate, who created documents for the bail, said he received two envelopes, one for himself and the other for the goons. His envelope contained his fees and a letter saying he must give the other one to those he is bailing. He read both the notes anyway. But it said someone was waiting for them at the Zero Degree bar. It turned out Mr. Sinha was the cover for some kind of trap. After hearing the advocate's side, Kirti was even more frustrated, "And you didn't try to find out?"

"I did. I followed them to the bar. But I don't know when and who met them there. After some drinks, they left. I asked them if anyone had met them, as I was the one who bailed them, but they refused to tell me anything, gave me some extra money thanking me. I didn't bother after that. I also had my things to do, so I could not follow them all along."

"You can go now," the detective had some clue now.

In the evening, a beautiful lady walked into the Zero Degree bar wearing a shirt and a pair of jeans that showed her lovely figure. Her hairs were tied in a ponytail but were long enough to reach down her shoulder. Kirti was twenty-five years beautiful girl. A few staring eyes fixed on her while the rest only enjoyed their drinks. She reached to the counter and asked for a drink. She looked at the person sitting behind the counter; he smiled and poured her a glass of red wine. The person with a nice mustache and beard with gloomy eyes smiled and asked, "What brought you here?"

"I need some information about these," and she threw two pictures on the counter.

As soon as he noticed the photos, he lifted them immediately and gestured for the lady to walk with him. She followed the person into the room. "Who killed them with this brutality?" The person asked, watching the photos as they entered the room. They were lying in a bloodbath and their mouths bloody. Their faces had changed their shapes, but he could recognize them. They were his regular customers.

"That's what brought me here." She replied. "Ask your staff to come over. I'll just take five minutes."

In a minute, the staff was standing in front of them. The pictures were shown to everyone, and the team recognized them. But nobody could remember if they had met someone. When Kirti lost her hope, another waiter came into the room asking for an apology for being late.

He remembered they didn't meet anyone, but he was the one to give them an envelope. A person walked into the bar in the evening wearing a cap, and the shadow almost covered his face. He offered some money to the waiter and handed him the envelope. After delivering the envelope, the waiter looked back, but the person was gone.

"How come you didn't see his face?" The person with the beard asked.

"Sir, he had his head down all the time, and when I was about to, the other customer called me, so... and he said it's just the business thing for them."

Kirti asked for the surveillance camera footage, but as described by the waiter, the person purposely had hidden his face. The detective sighed. Just another dead end! She left the bar without a word, wandering about the person who had given the envelope, providing the address to their death!

A Treasure!

Years ago, in 2007, after he became an orphan, Nihit left the town. He was only fourteen. The town he left behind had given him too much pain. He had lost his mother. He had lost his only friend. He even had to leave the girl he loved. Now he was in Vizag - the city of destiny. He had nothing in his pocket except a mouth organ his mother gifted him.

One night when he was sitting on the bench, past eleven, beneath the tree as the rain had started, reminiscing everything that happened to him, he was little tired. A group of boys appeared in front of him. He couldn't see their faces clearly, but almost all were teenagers, maybe seventeen to eighteen, just like him, an orphan. No! They were not like him; the only similarity between them was that they were orphans. They could not be like Nihit.

"Hey kid, what are you doing here?" one of them asked.

"Nothing, just..."

"Cut the crap, whatever you have, just give it to us," the other scoffed.

"I have nothing." Nihit replied calmly.

"You sure?" the third one barked, pointing to his shirt's pocket.

"If I had anything, I'd have given. Besides, I don't want to get beaten. For sure, I don't have anything." He took out the mouth organ from the packet, "As for this; it's worthless," he lied and put it in the pocket of pant safely.

This was the most valuable thing for him in this world, more than anything. His mother bought him this mouth organ. And after his mother left him, he had two treasures only, one he handed to the person he loved and trusted the most. The other one was a mouth organ!

The first boy grabbed the collar of Nihit's shirt. Nihit clenched his fists. "I don't lie!" he said, keeping his calm. For this thing in his pocket, he would lie till the end of the earth and wouldn't even count them in the world's lies. He spoke the truth. This was worthless for them who were asking for it, but not for him.

At this point, he sensed a hand approaching his face, just when it was about to hit him, the attack was blocked, and before he could react, Nihit blew a punch on his stomach. The boy groaned in pain. "Bastard! Face the trouble now!" the other one said. Nihit's face darkened; what he had to lose ultimately… A big nothing!

The two attacked simultaneously. He dodged the one, but another got his chest, making him lose his balance. Nihit fell on the ground straight backward, but the rain had softened the ground. He coughed a bit. The same boy, who gave him a blow, threw his feet, pointing at Nihit's chest, but Nihit rolled quickly, dodging the attack, and stood in a flash. He threw his eyes in all directions and suddenly ran, pushing the boy in front of him. The other two boys tried to catch him, "The hell, you want to escape now!" and ran behind him. Nihit stopped suddenly in less than 15 or 20 meters and picked up the wooden rod. The one behind him had no time to think about what he would do and got the blow in his stomach. "Aahhh…" he let out a scream.

Nihit could now see the horror in the eyes of the other boy. They didn't expect him to get hostile to this level. After all, they were just a bunch of teenagers who would bully the weaker ones or someone like Nihit who was alone. The ones under their age and looted them with whatever they had. They just had to slap a couple of times to get whatever they wanted. But this time, it was something they had never thought of.

As for the moment, the one standing ran backward, leaving the injured one groaning to the place. Nihit didn't hurt him further; neither did he chase the other one. The one who ran backward returned with the other boys, and they took the injured one. All vanished in a few minutes.

Nihit changed the place. He knew the place wasn't safe anymore. He didn't throw the wooden rod he had; this kept his safety ensured. He slipped into the dark, leaving enough space between the main road and the place he thought of getting a rest. He tried but couldn't sleep either, because of the rain. After some time, at around 3 am, he fell asleep; when the rain had stopped, he didn't know.

Not after a long time, less than three hours, someone jerked him. Nihit grabbed his rod and was about to hit the person before him.

"Hey, hey, watch it, boy!" the boy before him tried to protect himself, taking a few steps back.

Nihit loosened the grip of his rod. His eyes fell on the boy. He had a beer bottle in his hand, although he didn't seem like he was drunk. The excellent placement of the face organs had made him another good-looking guy the same age or a year older than him. "What do YOU want now?" Nihit almost spilled all of his anger on him.

"I don't want anything. Why are you so angry? Cool down, dude! Is there anything wrong?"

"Everything is!"

The boy before him didn't expect that answer, "Well, who are you?"

Nihit didn't answer for a long time.

"What are you doing here? Alone." he asked another question.

Before he could talk anymore, he saw Nihit grabbing his head and falling unconscious.

"Hey dude, what... what's happening?" he threw the bottle and grabbed Nihit. There was no time to think about anything. He brought Nihit to his house, less than 150 meters away. No one noticed; it was still dark outside.

Nihit could hear some noises, "Get some water first; I'll tell you later who he is." Nihit wanted to say something, but he had no strength. At the door, suddenly, the rod slipped through his hand and made some noise. The girl watched in surprise with big eyes. "What is that?!" she looked at her brother. "I don't know." the boy replied sincerely.

The boy put Nihit on the bed and checked if he had a fever by touching Nihit's forehead, and there was a slight fever. The boy thought he was in the rain the whole night, possibly that's why. His sister got a glass of water; splashed it on Nihit's face, but he didn't wake. "Let him sleep. If he is no better than now in a few hours, I'll call the doctor." The boy said, and his sister nodded. After some time, he got ready for work and left.

After three hours, about past nine-thirty in the morning, the sister thought to visit the guest. As she entered the room, she noticed that the guest was mumbling something in his sleep, she reached out to hear but couldn't understand what he was saying, and it seemed that he was having a nightmare in broad daylight. 'Something's troubling him', she thought. All of a sudden, he grabbed her hand, and she got scared. Sweat beads gathered on her forehead. "Lily... I. I.." This time, she could hear his words, and he loosened his grip over her wrist. That eased off her fear, and she sighed in relief. Her hand reached to her chest, trying to make her inhaling normal.

After another hour, her brother returned. "How's the guest?" he asked. "He is better than in the morning," she replied, "temperature seems normal." Both siblings talked about a few more things.

The two were talking when Nihit appeared in front of them. He looked nervous. He had questions in his eyes, he was thinking about something. "Hey brother," the boy reached out to help Nihit to sit at the dining table. "Take a sit first," he wanted Nihit to sit.

After a few more awkward seconds, the boy introduced himself, "I'm Jay, and this is my sister, Gayatri," Nihit glanced at the girl. The girl looked sweet, had a friendly smile on her face, and her long hairs were reaching to her waist.

"Why would you do this?" Nihit asked.

"We can discuss that later," Gayatri brought him a glass of water.

"The food is ready; you must be hungry." For no reason, she was concerned for the stranger she barely knew.

"I'm Nihit," He introduced himself and ate the food silently. While eating, the siblings didn't bother him with anything.

"Why would you do all this?" Nihit asked again.

"I don't know, I just..." Jay replied sincerely.

"When did you have the meal last time?" Gayatri asked him.

"Before three days, maybe."

No wonder he fell unconscious, she thought. "Why did you have the rod in your hand?" Gayatri asked with curiosity. Though, she killed her interest in Lily purposefully.

Nihit narrated the story of last night's fight with the boys and how he became an orphan. There was something else, too, he wanted to talk about, but he didn't. It's not the right time; I barely know them, he thought.

Gayatri felt sad for the boy. She could find the connection between them. Jay was thirteen years old when they lost their parents in the car accident, and Gayatri was fifteen. They had only each other now. Fortunately, they had their house. Gayatri wanted to leave her school and do something that could feed both siblings. But her brother Jay disagreed. She tried but couldn't find any valid point to turn the table around; he made her all the points' invalid one or the other way.

Jay promised her that he would continue his studies after 2-3 years once he thought everything was going well. Though he was younger, now he was the in-charge. He knew she was the elder one, but he was a brother and had to protect her. After all, they had each other only.

Three years had passed, she was eighteen, and he was sixteen. As promised, he had started school again and terminated full-time work into part-time.

HER Brother

At the time of leaving, Nihit couldn't talk of the compensation what they had done for him for two reasons. He had nothing to compensate with, was the first reason. And what they did was selfless, and after knowing their story, it would be disrespectful to their emotions to talk about the compensation.

"I think I should leave now," Nihit said after a few minutes. He didn't want to become a burden on them. Jay didn't say anything. Honestly, he didn't know what to say. He just looked at him with surprise in his eyes.

"But where will you go?" Gayatri was concerned.

"I don't know," Nihit replied after momentarily silence. "Thanks for everything, sister!" He had a sly smile. He meant it when he called Gayatri, sister. He remembered he had scared her by grabbing her hand. "Thanks, brother!" he said, looking at Jay and walked out of the door.

After he left, Gayatri gave Jay a look of dissatisfaction. "How could you let him go?" Gayatri scolded Jay. "Where will he go? What will he do? He is alone! He has nothing!"

He gave her a look in return, "what?!"

"Do something, stop him!" she was worried about Nihit.

Although Jay brought Nihit home, he was surprised by his sister. He was HER brother now, and nothing could change that fact, no matter what! Jay has to do something. He knew his sister. He sighed helplessly, waiving both his hands in the air. "Okay! I'll do something." He said and left the house.

It took Jay fifteen minutes to spot Nihit. He was sitting

at the table of a tea stall. Nihit knew he had nothing but searched for his pockets and was surprised to know that he could afford a tea. He took a few sips, and the rest of the tea was getting cold. He was long lost in his thoughts. What could be his thoughts? Maybe he was thinking about his mother; or maybe about the girl he loved and left behind. Maybe how he is going to survive in this cruel world; or maybe about the girl he called his sister a few moments ago, Gayatri.

Jay came slowly and sat beside Nihit without saying anything. As for now, he could understand Nihit's situation, both were almost the same age, and he knew what it felt to be like this. From the morning till noon, he guessed that Nihit doesn't talk much, which was an accurate guess. Nihit noticed when Jay sat beside him but didn't say anything.

"What is it?" Nihit asked after some time.

"Look, we can help you. You can stay with us."

"Why would you help? I'm a stranger. How could you trust me?"

"Because you're Gayatri's brother now, makes you my brother too. I may not trust you, but I trust her!" he looked in Nihit's eyes straight.

Nihit looked at him thoroughly. He guessed that Gayatri must have scolded Jay. He respected women but wouldn't call anyone sister out of nowhere for anything. That place needed to be earned for him, and Gayatri had done that. How? Only Nihit could tell that! When Jay returned with Nihit, Gayatri had a broad smile.

The next day when Jay was about to leave for his work, Nihit asked if Jay could help, finding him some work.

"Yeah, sure!" Jay had asked the manager of the paper

mill he worked at. Looking at his personality and attitude, he guessed Nihit wouldn't like to sit and eat. So the previous day, he had already asked the manager. He wasn't going to ask him straight to work, but he knew Nihit would ask for help, one or the other day. However, after the job was confirmed, Jay insisted that he should take a rest for at least a week because he was weak. Once Jay and Gayatri were convinced, they allowed Nihit to go to work.

Nihit was cold with his behavior. He spoke straightforwardly to everyone, at his work also. Even Jay would sometimes get scared of that stern look Nihit had in his eyes, even though he was the one who brought him to the house. Gayatri would call him brother. It didn't bother her that he was younger than her. With time, he started to open up with both the siblings. After two-three months, the bond between the three contained affection for each other.

But Nihit was close to Gayatri. Those days when he would have nightmares when Gayatri found him trembling in sleep during her night visits, she would sit beside him, holding his hand and that would ease off his pain.

Gayatri would get scared of the lightning and thunder when the rainy season was in its middle. She would walk to Nihit and wake him up. He would sit at her head, and she would sleep soundly. The following day, Jay would wake up and find Nihit asleep sitting and Gayatri head on his lap. Jay would smile but wouldn't disturb them.

One day Nihit had the day off and had nothing to do, so he went to pick up Gayatri from her college. As siblings talked while walking, a group of four boys surrounded them. Gayatri was scared slightly; the identical boys had tried to bully Nihit months back when Jay found him. He didn't remember all the faces, but he remembered the face which asked for his treasure. How could he forget that face?

"Girl, move aside; we have business with him," one of them said.

Nihit nodded to Gayatri, and she stood aside, worried for her brother. She wanted to stop this or help her brother, but there was no way out.

"Look, I have money now. Back then, I had nothing. You can get it and forget what happened." Nihit said flatly.

"That's not going to happen," the one who was injured last time spoke and threw the punch on Nihit's face. Nihit dodges the punch. The second guy threw the leg to his stomach; Nihit caught it and threw him back. The one who got injured last time was unfortunate this time too. Nihit looked at him and, Slap! Slap! His right cheek had fingers printed on it. Before he could retreat, another slap! This time his left cheek was red. Others were frightened because the eldest one was getting beaten. If he was getting beaten, how could others stand a chance? Despite being orphans and what happened before, they didn't get the lessons they should have taken already.

One of them grabbed Gayatri. As soon as Nihit heard Gayatri voice, his face darkened. His quiet, calm look had long gone, cold gaze returned to his eyes. His cream-colored frame could not hide the anger in them. He looked at the boy who held her. "Let her go," Nihit roared the loudest. Sweat gathered on the boy's forehead, and his grip loosened over Gayatri. Gayatri also was frightened looking at Nihit at this moment. She even could not look into his eyes. Nihit grabbed the collar of that boy and Slap! Slap! Slap! Slap!

Slap! Slap! Slap! "How dare you? This was between us!" he roared again. Slap! Slap! Slap! Slap! Slap! Slap! He didn't count. No one dared to move to save the boy. He continued till the boy spilled out a mouthful of blood. That's when Gayatri walked to Nihit and pulled his sleeve but didn't utter a word. Nihit let him go with another powerful slap, and the boy fell to the ground.

Nihit held Gayatri wrist gently and left the place as if nothing had happened.

That night at the dining table, only Jay was mainly talking. Gayatri would only answer whatever she was asked. Nihit barely spoke the word since they returned home. He even did not change his clothes. The black trouser and the light blue shirt, sleeves still folded to the elbow. Gayatri didn't dare to ask him to do anything. "The business isn't over yet," his mind chanted the phrase. He was going to leave the town next month or so, and he could not let his sister in danger.

The same night Nihit had a nightmare. Though Gayatri was horrified by the behavior of Nihit, she loved him. He did what he did for her sake; otherwise, he would let the boys go with just a couple of slaps. She sat and held his hand, "I'm here, okay! Everything's fine!" She rubbed his hand and stroked his head, "It's okay! Ssshhh... Sleep, I'm here by your side." She assured him. He mumbled for some more time and finally slept in peace. Gayatri fell asleep too, just sitting at her brother's head.

A figure walked to the seven-storied construction building at four in the morning. The sky was gurgling with the drums, and it was heavy raining with lightning outside.

At the construction site, three figures were sleeping;

one of the sleeping three had difficulty in sleeping. He was injured badly. Three were awake, the elder teenager and two adults. The group was of six. There was a fireplace, and the cold wind was blowing because of the rain. They sat around the fire, making a circle. "Who was he?" One of the adults asked. "We met him near the bridge for the first time in the night around a month or two ago." The teenager replied and narrated the story of that night. "You know where he lives?" another adult asked. "Near the paper mill factory," the teenager replied. While discussing, they heard someone approaching them. They watched the direction and waited till the other party arrived.

They could not see his face. The other party just arrived and stood still, didn't say anything. Even after a minute when the figure stood still, one of them asked, "Who the hell are you? What are you doing here at this hour?" But the figure still didn't say a word. Hearing their partners talking to someone other than the group, they all woke up with sleep in their eyes.

The lightning struck after some time, and the figure was visible. The person was young, rather, a boy with handsome and a calm face. But his eyes had killing intents, besides; he was holding a weapon - a gun. The boys recognized his face and understood what he was doing at this hour. "You want to die or what? Let us sleep." One of the adults scoffed, noticing the weapon.

The person pointed out the gun to those two who were adults. Two gunshots between the eyes before they could blink or think of anything, the person turned to the four boys. They were frightened already, sweating. As soon as the figure turned to them, all froze to death, not even daring to move an inch. Why not? Someone just appeared from nowhere and had killed their masters without any mercy. Who will save them now? Their faces turned pale. His cold eyes were fierce. One of them started crying, "Don't kill us, please!" A figure reached out, and there was a crisp sound. Slap!

"You all have only chance. Leave the town as soon as possible!" The voice was calm but authoritative. The figure stepped back, turned, and stood for a moment in the rain. The drops reaching to the ground through the gunpoint was another warning and the figure left without looking back.

The next morning's newspaper had shocking news for the townspeople.

As for those boys, they vanished into the air. No one was bothered about them; no one knew about them either. Not even before the news. After all, they were orphans.

After another month or so, Nihit left Gayatri and Jay, promising he would be back.

The Trail

Detective Kirti reached the city's south again with her subordinate at the murder site. She observed the walls of the wagons; everything was red. The wagon had bents on its borders. They were smashed into the walls too. What a monster! Nothing new than the first time she visited. But when she reached her vehicle to return, she noticed something. The car tire marks. She asked her subordinate to look for it and report her.

The forensic department reported that tire marks were of the Mercedes-Benz CLS. 'A rich bird', she thought. Kirti's subordinate provided the information that there were twelve owners of that same model and all of the owners had their alibis - except one.

When she asked for the tire marks, she didn't only mean for tire marks. After working with her for almost four years, the subordinate knew what she wanted to know when she asks for something.

"And who is that?" The detective asked.

"Shirish Ahuja." The subordinate provided the information. "A twenty-eight-year-old former CEO of ARK textiles. He wasn't home, and neither was he in his office. Nor at the regular bar he visits."

"Where he was then?" she asked.

"No one knows yet. I think it's time to meet Mr. Shirish," The subordinate said.

* * *

"Why am I even getting interrogated?" The CEO wasn't

ready to co-operate with her.

"We found two dead bodies, Mr. Shirish, lying in the bloodbath! And we suspect you are involved." Kirti said, staring at him.

"What nonsense! And why would you make me a suspect out of nothing?" He rose from his chair, pressing his fists on the glass table.

"The tire marks we found on the site matches your car." Kirti said calmly.

"There are a bunch of cars of the same makes of the tire in the city. You can ask them," he replied arrogantly.

"Where were you on 1st January, in the evening, specifically at 6:20 pm?"

His face turned pale, realizing something about the day. "Wherever I was, I did not commit that!"

"Well, that makes our doubt more powerful, Mr. Shirish. If you want it simple and straight, it can be. But if you want something else, don't blame me for the consequences." Kirti warned him, but she looked calm.

"I was with a friend," he replied.

"Name, please... Can they give a statement?" Kirti asked.

As expected, Kirti was not surprised to learn the fact that he was with one of his girlfriends. Besides, a person like Shirish could not do that; whatever he does, he doesn't like to get personally involved in such things as murders. Moreover, looking at his physique, he couldn't break bones by just hitting anyone. Someone was more potent than that of Mr. Shirish. Someone with real skills...

When Kirti walked out of his office, he dialed a number, "Brother, I think it's going to be tough. I thought it would be just another inspector, but it's her, detective Kirti. You know her already!"

"Don't worry. I can afford to mess with anybody in this city!" The voice came from another end before the call got disconnected.

The detective sat on her chair in the police station, playing with the pen in her right hand. Her face looked calm, but her eyes didn't agree with her posture. While thinking, the subordinate didn't disturb her and looked at the documents on the table before him. After investigating for almost half of a month, to get nothing, she was frustrated. The ordinary goons were murdered for nothing. No one could have the benefits if thought. It looked like murders in internal rivalries of local gangs, but still at the level of crossing brutality. Because they were not just murdered; they had dislocated arms, broken bones, and ribs. They were tortured for something before getting killed. There was zero evidence. No fingerprints, no weapon at the site, no DNA, no link to connect to any person, nothing with anyone that could have a solid motive to kill someone with such kind of brutality.

As for the one who was robbed, Kirti concluded that he was just a pawn. 'Maybe, someone's trying to mislead us', she thought. 'Whatever we have is not enough! There must be something else, something more…'

But when her subordinate and other sources failed to find anything even after a month, there was only one thing to do; to close the case due to a lack of evidences. But she could not let this happen. Whoever did this might be planning his subsequent murder, if any. Besides, she could not let a criminal live his life peacefully.

　　　　　　　　　　　　　　　　　　　The Whistler

It took her six years to get the tag of Detective, because she thought like one. Before officially getting into the police department as an ACP, Kirti had helped the police department solve cases that were difficult to be solved at one glance. She had helped the department in one of the cases that happened in her college, two girls went missing from her college, and she had a chance to help the police department. After that, she decided what she wanted to do in her life. When she was twenty in 2013, a serial killer had headlined on the front page of every newspaper for nine murders for half a year at least, and she was the one to detect a particular pattern and probable next target of the killer in a month. In 2014, when she was twenty-one, she helped with the significant threat of bombing the entire city. Which was plotted by the terrorists, but later turned out that it was the local MLA's son who was gambling with the drug racket.

After joining officially as an ACP in 2016, she solved many complex cases in her six-year career. And if she could not do anything about this case, it would be shameful for her, for the fact that this would be the first case of her career she could not solve. As for the time being, there were no murders after that massacre, but her guts had bad feelings about this, terrible feelings!

When she was at the edge of losing hope, there was an anonymous call from a girl. The voice said Kirti should check the whereabouts of the goons and an incident on 2nd August at the Seminary Hills. The voice was of a strong lady. It wasn't any sacred girl or someone messing around. The lady had a tone of some command in her voice. After the Intel provided, call was disconnected.

"What is it with the Seminary Hills? And what's so

interesting about 2nd August?" Kirti wasn't sure about the call, but she was almost going to close the case; even if it could be shameful for her, she was left with this option only. As her last hope, she gave it a try, and the subordinate found it.

"A Murder...!" The subordinate provided the information after she asked him to verify the call, "a murder happened on that same day on the Seminary Hills. And surprisingly, the two people we found dead were there."

"And you don't think that's just another coincidence, do you?"

"I don't." he replied.

"Let's find out then." Kirti said.

"Looks like your guts had it, Detective. And if your theory of torture is true, then I think we are walking into a blunder..."

The subordinate had already talked about the case with inspector Das, who was in charge of the murder case which happened on the Seminary Hills. Kirti and her subordinate were at the police station of Seminary Hills in another half an hour.

She could have gotten the information on her table but she wanted to get involved personally and know the details of the case. Inspector Das was handling two cases at the time. But neither case could reach at any conclusion. The first one was Kayra Raman. She was murdered in a broad daylight in the crowd on 2nd August, yet the killer was in the wind. The other case was three murders on the city's outskirts, a month and a half before Kayra's.

Two things got Kirti's attention in both cases inspector Das was working on. In Kayra's case, people related to her. And in the second case, the pattern used for the murders. The pattern used by the killer was the same as the wagons now, the case on which Kirti was working, with the same brutality. The broken ribs and bones, several wounds, and the center of the attack - the heart.

When the list of people related to Kayra's case came into her hand, she immediately asked for the Mercedes-Benz CLS car owners list. There was one common name on the list of owners of the cars, and in the case of Kayra Raman. Kirti felt uneasy since she was familiar with that common name, and the person. The subordinate could notice her being uneasy, but he didn't say anything.

The tour to the Seminary Hills police station was worth it!

When Kirti and her subordinate reached back to the police station, her cell rang, and she did not even have a chance to climb down the car. There was another murder! She reached the crime scene only to see the same horror of red color everywhere, with a dead body lying on the floor. The pattern was as ruthless as the previous case, or maybe much more brutal and horrific than before. After seeing the condition of the dead body, the subordinate stood few moments and could not control himself. He ran straight outside of the room to vomit.

When the subordinate was normal and returned to his proper senses, Kirti blurted, "Check for the connections between the last victims and this one…." She had already speculated that this was the next one on the list. The subordinate looked at her trying to wave off the thoughts of Kirti's theory. Someone was trying to extract something from them before killing; what could it be? With the name she had, her theory was way too much complicated now…

A Ruined Date

In the late afternoon, he sat thinking about nothing but her! Nihit stared at the walls and the rays of light coming through a window. As the cigarette in his hand reached to his fingers and he could sense the heat, that's when he returned to reality. He threw out the filter and sat still, remembering the lecture he had attended of Engineering Graphics.

Five months back, sitting in the second last seat at the final stage of his drawing, Nihit felt a gaze on him. He turned around, and there she was, looking at him. She had sparkling eyes with a hint of innocence and curiosity, but one could tell that those beautiful eyes had seen the injustice of life. A small bindi between her eyes and a strand of her curly hair touching her cheek made her look even more gorgeous than she was. One would love to fall for her. Suddenly she was startled and fixed her eyes on the drawing she was trying to complete. She couldn't focus on it. Her curly hairs were covering her right temple, and an unexpected blush ran through her lips. Nihit tried to ignore it, returned his eyes to his business, and completed it.

He mostly sat in Engineering Graphics and Mathematics lectures and wouldn't attend other classes. In another Engineering Graphics lecture, he could still sense the gaze almost after a week, but he was sure about the person this time. He looked at her, but this time she did not look away; her eyes were asking for help. He glanced at the drawing sheet before her, took a few moments, and gestured her with his hand to turn the protector around. She followed him, looking at his hand gestures that led her to nowhere. He frowned helplessly and took her copy himself, followed some steps, didn't use the eraser even a single time, and never put the pencil down till the job was completed, took hardly three minutes, and returned the copy. She watched his every move with several blinks, her lips curled into a slow smile.

After the lecture, she took the initiative to ask him. "Would you like to have a coffee with me?" She had a slight hesitation. Nihit felt her voice had a slight friction in it, which Nihit thought was sweet.

"No!" he replied in a flash.

How could he do that? How could he reject a beautiful girl like her? Who does that? Who the hell does he think he is? But she awkwardly accepted his rejection with a wry smile as she had no other choice. Now that she had it, she knew why girls don't approach him. His behavior drives them away; needless to say, girls were frightened because of the way his eyes looked at everything and everyone - with coldness.

"How about I have a tea and you get a coffee?" he looked into her eyes with the same cold expression. Her eyes glittered again, and she smiled unconsciously. "That will do. Alright!" she was excited.

"Five thirty in the evening would be a nice time! What's your name?" He asked

"Kayra." and that's where the conversation ended. He just turned around and left all of a sudden. She felt dejected for a moment. But stood there watching him go, clutching the book to her chest tightly.

Surrounded by the greenery outside the city, it was a nice place to be called the Green café. She was unsure if he

        The Whistler

would appear, but she decided to wait. Though he had left suddenly, he had accepted the proposal over tea. The place was well known because that was the only coffee shop near Wilson College.

When Nihit arrived, he wasn't on time but wasn't too late either. She smiled at him as he entered the coffee shop, but his expression didn't change. Kayra could observe the hesitation in his eyes. But she couldn't say why. A few minutes later, his tea was over, but they didn't talk. He ordered another tea. And she could see the disgust in his eyes while sipping it. Her curly hairs were touching her cheek, and he tried his best to avoid the distraction.

"Would you mind if I ask something?"

"You like to interview people or what?" he replied.

"I didn't mean that way... I was just curious about you." She smiled hesitantly.

What does he even mean? It was kind of a date, and she wasn't even allowed to ask him something. Anything? At all?

"Why would you be?"

"What?" She was puzzled.

"Curious. About me…"

"Oh, that... because, you don't talk much."

"I know that!" he was still cold.

It looked like a kind of heated argument just for nothing. She was curious just now. But because of the rapid change in his cold behavior, she knew he wouldn't talk anymore. Looking at him, anyone could tell that he wasn't in a good mood. The awkward silence lasted a few more minutes, and they were out of the coffee shop.

She was also kind of a silent person, so there were no long conversations. She could think of many topics to talk about, with him. She could ask him where he came from and why he would not speak much. She could talk about his personality she had observed from the day her eyes fell on him or about his calm and quiet nature that frightened everyone around. She could appraise his knowledge or tell him that he looked handsome in his cream-colored frames that many girls could die for him that he was the topic of gossip in her hostel. But she did not talk any of this.

Her hostel was about just five or six hundred meters away. She didn't know if she should ask him to walk her to the hostel, so she just stood and didn't say anything. Concluding all this, she knew that she had ruined the date. Wait, how did she ruin it? It was him. The evening had passed, and street lamps were glowing on the poles between the trees. She stood with watery eyes on the verge of crying. Just when she knew he would leave and she'll be all alone, he said something. "We had it, now you can leave."

Finally, she had nothing to do but cry!

"But, I would like if you accompany me." He said, looking into her teary eyes. "To that tea stall." he pointed with the gesture of his eyes at the distance of around 150 meters.

Wearing a blue shirt and knee-length skirt, her few curly hairs on her face and rest open to her back, she looked beautiful. But to her unfortunate, he didn't seem to notice any of it. She strolled with him. The tea stall was on the same way to her hostel. It was near another street lamp pole and beneath a large tree. The light rays were passing through the leaves.

"A coffee and a tea." he ordered, "and one Marlboro." he asked for the cigarette.

"You like the roadside tea at the stall than that of the coffee shop?" she asked slowly.

He nodded and then followed the awkward silence again. She didn't expect him to talk much as she knew him now, but she wanted that this date shouldn't be a disaster. Though it was going to be one, it didn't.

"You are looking sweet," He finally noticed it. He had noticed her expression since they met; he had seen her joyful face looking at him, and he had caught her watery eyes when he coldly told her to leave. He had noticed her round earrings and the strand of hair that distracted him.

"Thanks!" she accepted his appraise; she knew he wouldn't say it but did. "Well, I wanted to thank you for one more thing."

"What's that?"

"You helped me in that lecture!"

Nihit just nodded, and she knew he welcomed her. He looked at her and said in a low tone, "I apologize for this." he took a lighter in his hand and turned his face the other way.

"It's alright!" she smiled slowly. She wouldn't like him smoking but didn't mind anyway. Besides, she knew no other person would have apologized to her for that.

After sipping the coffee and tea, both strolled towards her hostel. While walking, he stopped suddenly and said, "Wait here!"

She looked at him and followed what he said. He walked outside the road into the dark, and a minute later, he returned with something in his hand, Lily flowers. "This is for you!"

he handed her with a gentle smile. She hadn't seen him smile before, not even once since the day she had noticed him. He would attend only two lectures and leave. Sometimes he would leave in between the lecture and never return. To her surprise, no professor ever bothered to ask him about that.

"Is this your first time?" she asked and couldn't help but blush.

"Isn't yours too?!" To read people with their behavior was one of his capabilities.

She nodded politely, and her smile widened. A few minutes later, both reached the gate of her hostel. She waved him bye, but he didn't. 'So cold!' She thought of his behavior for a moment but didn't mind and admired him. The gate closed behind her, and she could hear someone blowing the whistle. Her lips curled into a wide smile listening to the whistle.

At a distance, in the dark, a pair of eyes spied them both since the moment they had met.

The Lost Love

Nihit would walk Kayra to her hostel every day after college hours, adding a few more minutes to their walk by stopping at the tea stall. He would not be in college mostly. But by the end of the day, he would be there for her. She didn't ask him where he was or why does he do whatever he do but silently miss him when he wasn't there.

"You don't look like younger than my age?" The other day after college, when Nihit walked Kayra to her hostel, he asked her at the tea stall. He guessed this might be an offending question to any woman, but that didn't bother him. The only thing which bothered him at the time was the name of the girl in front of him. He had a past with this name.

Instead of getting offended, she told him with a smile while sipping a coffee, "A year older than you, twenty-six." She knew his straight-forwardness. "Some family issues got me here late." she provided more information. "Why would you ask? Is there something wrong with that?" her eyes panicked while some thoughts made their way through her mind.

"No!" his cold expressions returned suddenly. I just wanted to confirm, he thought himself. He slipped his hand into his pocket and took the mobile out, wrote something, and sent it to the contact named Karan.

Karan was the only one Nihit could count on besides Jay in the college. Nihit knew Karan from the first day itself. Jay had introduced them. Jay and Karan have been friends for five years. Nihit didn't know anyone in the college, so he was left with Karan. It's been months, and Karan had helped

Nihit in almost everything he could. May it be arranging the meeting with the college authorities or helping him find his favorite class. For the fact, Jay had told Karan that Nihit is not a student and comes to the college for business purposes.

Though Nihit didn't talk much, they had an excellent understanding. Unlike others, he wasn't afraid of Nihit's stern look ever. As for Nihit, it's been a decade since he could find someone with the same personality as him, who could think precisely like him. Karan was someone whose actions would align with his words. Karan reminded him of an old friend Nihit once had when he was a teenager. He looked like that old friend too, a little, but Nihit didn't give it another thought. While he would cross-check everyone's background before working with them, Karan was the exception. Karan did an outstanding job when it came to looking out for someone or something if he was asked. And that's what he usually did for Nihit. Nihit could only trust Karan with such things.

"Kayra Raman. She is from Bhubaneswar, upbringing by a single mother. Nine years ago left the city and settled in a small town near Vizag. Four years ago, her mother also passed because of an illness. Her uncle, her mother's brother, is responsible for being her backer. Well, she gets the scholarship with her intelligence to support her education.

Before leaving the town, she was devastated for someone, a boy. They say she wasn't ready to leave the town. But her mother's illness left her with no choice. She still visited the town every year till two years back. And after that, she didn't seem to know any other boy in her life except you." He paused, "Well, what she likes and not you can find out by yourself!" A week later, when Karan met Nihit, he provided the information. Karan didn't know the boy he just

                                    The Whistler

mentioned, was standing before him.

Nihit carefully listened and nodded while playing with the cigarette in his right hand. He hadn't sent Karan to know about her relationships; he just wanted to clarify if it was the same girl. But Karan said everything in just one go, so now he had the information. "There's one more thing." Nihit said after listening to him.

"That is?" Karan asked casually.

"Someone's spying!"

Karan didn't need more of anything. These kind things would always thrill him when he was asked for. Now that he had something interesting again, he was excited. However, he looked concerned for Nihit and Kayra, who could spy on them... And for what purpose...

When Kayra strolled with Nihit to her hostel, she would hold his arm hesitantly and continue her nonsense chatter. Nihit didn't mind Kayra holding his arm. After all these years, Nihit was with the one he had loved his entire life. While lighting the cigarette, he would look into her eyes and didn't light it; or sometimes, he seemed like he didn't care at all. But he wouldn't talk much, so whenever she wanted to hear a compliment from him, she would wear a shirt neither loose nor tight and a knee-length skirt and let her little curly hair open to play with the wind. In those months, both were getting closer day by day.

That evening when they met, college was off, but he was still there. It was already dark when they met this evening as he was late. Near the hostel, in the dark corner, he stood with Kayra after he had walked her to the hostel. "There is a thing I want to tell you." Kayra said. He nodded in affirmation.

"There was a boy in my town, and I wanted to marry him. He promised me he would. But one day, he was not there. Ten years ago, he just disappeared." she said while a few drops gathered in her beautiful eyes.

He reached out for her waist and pulled her slowly towards himself. He looked straight into her eyes. She blinked a several times and returned the water from her eyes. Her heart had started beating faster because of his sudden action, her breath getting heavier and heavier, her chest touching his, with abnormal inhaling. His right hand slowly moved from her temple to her hairs. "You have me," he said in a whisper, leaned a little and his lips reached to the corner of hers, his hand caressing her hairs. She wrapped her hands around his neck. After both were almost out of a breath, that's when they let it go.

* * *

Somewhere in the city, in the room of a wooden house, there was a dead silence. The cold wind blew in between with a bit of humming, and the dim light in the room illuminated enough light that one could see things correctly. A person sat facing the window on a chair, smoking. The other one stood behind the chair; he had just arrived.

The sitting person threw the photo of a beautiful girl on the table, "Get this one!"

The standing person looked at the photo and said, "Why in the world would you kill this beauty?" The upright person had a beard.

"That doesn't matter to you. Get the money and just

do your job. I want her dead. Make sure she doesn't escape and don't mess around." The person sitting in the chair said authoritatively.

"Consider it's done!" the bearded person replied, picked up the photo, and left the place.

The next day was nice; winter had its charm. In the afternoon, a black Luxury car stopped near the hostel. It was the custom-colored graphite black 1950cc beauty with 245 Horsepower, a Mercedes-Benz CLS. Kayra just stepped out of the gate and didn't bother to give it a thought to who might have come in the car but still was curious about who does drive this beautiful car. That's when she saw him stepping out of the driving seat, wearing cream-colored frame glasses. He looked handsome in the sky blue shirt with black collar lining and trousers, sleeves rolled up till the elbow, and a nice watch on his left hand. Although he wore like this only, he looked different today. "Kayra," he called her out. Kayra looked at him with big eyes, opening her mouth and her hand reaching to cover her mouth.

"What, you own this thing?!" she asked in disbelief.

"Looks like you don't trust me," he said with a smile.

"Hey, it's not like that! You never drove this to the college." she giggled.

He reached out and opened the door for her. She sat inside with a broad smile, and he closed the door. As he headed to the driving seat, he felt uneasy. He could feel eyes on him. He stood for a moment and didn't move. Then he slipped his hand into his pocket and took the cell out. He called Karan, said something, and hung up the call. He sat inside and ignited the car. The engine of the black beauty roared, and a vehicle headed towards the city.

"Where are we going?" she asked him.

"To meet someone." he replied.

After driving almost for an hour, a small town arrived. To Kayra, the road was familiar. As the distance was getting lesser, her heartbeats were increasing.

The car stopped at the café outside the city. The place was nice. Except for a few glassworks, the cafe looked like it was built by the woods. The tables were placed underneath the giant trees. The main road was less than 30 meters. Behind the café, a Brooklet flowed, and a few tree leaves floated with it. It was a quiet place. There wasn't much crowd. They sat at one of the corner tables and ordered a coffee for Kayra, a tea for Nihit, and some snacks. He was hungry, so obviously, she was too.

"Whom are we going to meet, by the way?" she asked again.

"Mother!" he replied slowly. "It's been a long time I haven't seen her."

"What! Why didn't you tell me before?" she was surprised. She blushed unconsciously, thinking he would introduce her to his mother. "And why wouldn't you meet her for a long time?" she asked.

"It's like..., I left the town long ago."

Kayra could feel the pain in his eyes under that cream-colored frame while he was talking about his mother. But she wasn't sure if that was a pain. But she was pretty happy that Nihit had opened his heart to her.

"How is she?" she asked about his mother.

Nihit didn't reply to that.

"How will she react?" She was nervous a bit at the point; she looked down at herself.

He just responded with a smile.

When they were full and were about to leave, the cafe manager approached Nihit, and to Kayra's surprise, he talked to him with the utmost respect even though he was older than Nihit.

"How does he know you?" When the manager left, she asked.

"I... run a business." he replied.

"Okay, that explains your car and why you don't attend lectures. But you attended a few lectures...."

"Out of curiosity, just to kill the time when I visited the college." he replied.

"Okay." A smile appeared on her face realizing that he visited the college every evening only for her. "Anyways, the café is beautiful, the place, the brooklet, the huts and arrangement beneath the trees..."

"You liked the place?" he asked.

"I loved it!" she replied.

He owned the café and the place. This was the first café he built when he started his business.

The Gambler

Nihit was fourteen when he left his hometown, leaving behind the only person he loved and who loved him back, Kayra. Further, he had Jay and Gayatri as his family, but he left them too in a short time and reached Kerala. Initially, he worked in restaurants and a newspaper agency; he needed to survive. Now that he knew the world is cruel, he has to look out for himself.

When he returned from work, he would reach outside the Martial arts class and observe it. With an empty pocket, he could not enter inside. Maybe, the Master could have made an exception and trained him without asking for any money, but Nihit didn't want that.

For a year, he observed it and practiced those moves in his room. During that period, he made a friend, Akriti, who helped him throughout his training by himself. She was one of the brightest students in the class of Martial arts.

After practicing for more than a year, he was skilled with the Kalari, the ancient Martial arts of India. Originally it was combat training, which combines weaponless self-defense, stamina exercise, and battle with dangerous metal weapons. In addition, it provides excellent fitness and strength to the body.

There are four stages of this art, Meithari, Kolthari, Ankathari, and Verumkai. In his self-training, his strength increased drastically, and the speed he achieved was remarkable. As for his age, he had achieved more than anyone could succeed in six or seven years. After that, he finally visited the Martial arts class when he had some money.

He hosted and participated in many dangerous campaigns, and saved people's lives. Looking at this average-looking boy with a lean body, no one could predict what kind of skills he possessed. After that, he still practiced everything for the next five years until he almost mastered the art and no ordinary person could stand before him; and then, one day, he reached the pinnacle; he mastered the art.

He was in the wind for the next five years, untraceable; nobody knew where he was!

Five years later, he returned to Vizag and worked in the library. He loved books and mathematics. He spent most of his time reading fiction and solving mathematics in the library. One fine day he selected a business category just for a change of the topic, and something got his interest. He researched things about it, made calculations, and finally, he was sure he wanted to do it. He wanted to start a business.

But there was a problem - money. He was good with the numbers, and had something in his mind but that was risky and could be considered as illegal and a crime. If he were caught, that would put him into the jail; no one likes and wants that. But then, he was ready to gamble. His brain reminded him he would go to the jail if he were caught. As for the fact, he would back off the gamble once his primary motive was achieved and run the business honestly.

However, he could not do it alone. He needed a partner!

Ritvik was his first and only friend in the city of Vizag. Nihit didn't talk much to people, but with him, wavelengths had matched. He met him one night while returning to his room from the library and had saved him from getting loot from the goons with the skills he had, when Ritvik was drunk. Later they became friends. Ritvik worked in the garage. Since there would be a crowd in the library only in the morning and evening, Nihit agreed to the idea that he would work with Ritvik in the garage for a few hours of the day.

He first learned basic things, observed mostly, and eventually learned all the parts of an automobile, how they work, and what their functions are. He fell in love with the cars!

And then, one day after walking out of the library, he was there with this crazy idea!

Ritvik laughed out wholeheartedly when he told his idea to start a business, "I like the spirit, by the way!" He said once he was done with laughing. "What are you planning to do? Whatever you're planning to do, needs the money. A lot of money! So just forget it!"

"I have a plan… But I need a partner! Just hear me out once." Nihit tried to convince Ritvik that they would go to the bank for the loan.

"For sure sir! You think the bank will give you a loan like you're their son-in-law!" Ritvik said with a frown.

"No! I have another thing for that matter too!" said Nihit.

"What is that thing?" Ritvik said, narrowing his eyes.

"Look, I need someone I can trust, not just any random freak out there."

"Go ahead..." Ritvik said.

"We'll approach a bank for the loan. The proposal and documents I create will ensure they won't get rejected. Maybe, they'll think twice about it, but here is the thing..."

Nihit paused.

"And that is..." Ritvik stared at him.

"If the loan is rejected, to avail the loan, we will give an offer to the manager that he might not refuse, in the name of some anonymous person. If the manager accepts the offer, we get the loan. If he reports to the police, he had already received the offer by the anonymous person."

"Dude, that is not cool. Stop pretending to be a godfather or something. You'll make an offer he can't refuse?" Ritvik chuckled.

"Might not ref...," Nihit replied awkwardly with a low tone.

"Damn your things and plans! Just don't play around the bush. Tell me everything, all the plans combined." Ritvik said.

It was simple! They would approach three different banks and ask for the loan for a business. If the manager or whoever is the head refused the loan proposal, they would offer him a sum or a share with an anonymous name. Whether the loan proposal was accepted or not, plan B of the anonymous offer depended on that. But in both the cases, accepted or rejected, they were getting the money they wanted, unless they were not getting it, at all!

They will get a loan from the first bank and invest the money in the business. The second loan they have sanctioned and in their pocket will pay the EMIs of the first one. The third one will be the backup and will be used to pay the EMIs of the second one and vice versa. They will get at least four to five long years in all this time.

The amount of the first loan they invested will give an

output from five or six months after they invested. Once they achieve their primary motive, they will soon pay off their loans and close all of the fake accounts. The game has begun, they will have a clean business, and now they can run it honestly.

Ritvik was stunned to hear what Nihit was saying and shocked to learn that something like this could hit his mind. Whatever he was telling was just unbelievable. "Holy shit...! Have you planned completely to go behind the bars? May God save me! I'm not in all the bulshit you just said!" Ritvik said glancing at Nihit and Nihit just looked back at him without saying anything.

"Well, what if the business does not work?" Ritvik was curious.

Nihit took a moment and said, "It will!" He was sure with his numbers, calculations, and his vision.

"Okay, now that I know you can create fake documents, how do I know you are using your real identity right now? How can I trust you?"

"I think I haven't done anything yet, that you cannot trust me!"

"But you didn't do anything either, that I can trust you!" Ritvik grinned at Nihit.

"Ugh..." Nihit sighed, realizing the sarcasm and what Ritvik meant. But he didn't have an answer to that, as whatever Ritvik said was making sense. However, Ritvik knew enough about Nihit and what kind of person he was; hence Ritvik was sure enough that he could trust the person before him. There was a silence for a few minutes, and finally, he said, "Alright! Done with this life with no money, but what if we get caught?"

"You're using what if while asking me the question!" Nihit replied, looking at him.

"So, you have another backup plan too?"

"Sort of!" Said Nihit. He did not have it!

They stood facing the Eastern Urban bank in the next fifteen days. Ritvik looked exactly like Nihit wanted him to. His enough grown physique and muscles while working in the garage made him look like a good-looking guy in the black and white suit. Nihit had chosen the outfits wisely in which Ritvik looked descent.

As they stood, Ritvik had a few drops of sweat on his forehead. He took the handkerchief and wiped it. "I don't believe I'm doing this for the sake of you, moron," he said with nervousness and glanced at Nihit. Nihit, too, seemed to be thinking something; he was nervous too. All depended on Ritvik now, whether they had a chance to get the loan or not.

The person sitting on the manager's chair was a middle-aged person with thick glasses on his eyes. His face was egg-shaped, and he looked like a tough man to deal with. But he wasn't, he spoke very well which increased the confidence of Ritvik, who had initially less courage in whatever he was doing.

"How much money would you need?" The manager asked.

"Three lakh," Ritvik said without blinking, and the manager noticed the confidence in the eyes of the boy.

"What business are you planning to do? Is the amount sufficient?" he asked, leaning his back to his chair, thinking that the money they asked was not very much, as he was doubtful if it was enough for any business.

Nihit opened a file and explained the business terms, deliberately revealing the numbers and the profit. The manager glanced at Ritvik. Ritvik explained that Nihit was his companion and was good with numbers. He avoided telling that he was the partner, as anyone could guess both were working together but still could doubt as Nihit looked much younger than needed. He talked everything on point. The manager glanced at Nihit suspiciously. "What if it doesn't work? How will you repay the debt to us?"

Nihit had worked hard on his script, along with Ritvik. They had gone through all the possible counter questions one could get asked while asking for the business loan. They were prepared for everything, the documents or the photographs of the site and all that stuff; they had gone through it multiple times.

"Sir..." Nihit explained a few more things showing the documents of the land they had, in which Ritvik's father had given it, in Ritvik's name, which was the back-up, if the business did not work. There was a death certificate also.

The manager liked the attitude of the duo and the confidence they had. Moreover, the amount they were asking was not much. The manager looked at the documents carefully and didn't find anything fishy. "Alright, let's see what I can do for you two." The manager said, and both left the cabin while the manager stared at them till both were out of the bank.

Nihit's research and calculations were accurate; and to their fortune, the first meeting went well. Ritvik couldn't stop laughing at what they had done when they stopped at the roadside tea stall. "How did you end up thinking like that?" Ritvik asked. "The library…!" Nihit replied.

They did the same things in the following weeks with another two banks. Now that Ritvik had gained confidence, he was less nervous or so. Those meetings too went nice; fortunately, they didn't have to use plan B of giving the offer in the name of an anonymous person, which was way too risky.

They had all three loans in their pocket in the next six months. Total nine lakhs!

They took the land on a lease outside the city's crowded area. Nihit chose the place. He had decided the site long ago, his research included everything. He was going to do a business with the café and Ritvik didn't doubt his decisions anymore. They deliberately avoided the concrete and brick work for the building. They used wood and glass. The laminated glass could cover almost half of the wall, and the rest would be wood. Only the foundation and the necessary columns were concrete. There was a risk of termite and the rain, but they had thought about it too. They provided the folding shields to use in the rainy season and the utmost possible things to avoid termites. The Brooklet flowing behind the cafe made it more delightful place, they took the advantage of that asset too.

The place was near the road that people should notice but not necessarily close enough that the dust would reach the café. Soon enough, people started to notice the café; people passing by would stop for some rest for themselves and their vehicles. They paid attention to the quality of the beverages, foods, and snacks. They provided it with the utmost of its best quality.

They kept the prices low for their services, but ensured that the profit of their calculated margin would not be hampered. The staff they used there was with Ritvik's contacts, and they could trust that their business would not be affected by those working people.

In less than a year, their hard work paid them back. The time flew by, and soon they had another café on the other side of the city. They calculated the crowd and future possibilities to not to get in any legal trouble. They spread it to the different parts of the town, plus the nearest cities, which worked too. Next, Nihit approached educational institutes and business buildings to offer the service in their cafeteria. The business grew larger and larger. Soon they paid their loans back and closed the fake bank accounts. Now that they had everything and their gamble worked, there was nothing to look back.

They had started it with a fraud, but their intentions were not wrong! Who doesn't want money? But they kept only enough money that was necessary for them to own their own houses and cars! They decided to donate the rest of the profit to the orphanages. Who would know being an orphan with no shelter to live with empty pockets better than these two?

Out of all, Nihit sometimes sat at the first café he built near his old town. That place was his favorite of all. The distance to his old town was hardly an hour's travel, where his mother waited for him, but he never visited her. He would reminisce about something while sitting at one of the tables and watching the flowing Brooklet. Ritvik had asked

Nihit many times, but he wouldn't tell and change the topic to their business.

One fine evening, when he was lost in his thoughts, someone tugged his sleeve, and a sweet face got his attention. Since that day, he would visit his café, this place, every day. That evening, Ritvik saw him smiling almost for the first time since they met. There was someone special in his life now.

The crowd there seemed it belonged to him, but it did not. Often a person would approach him to talk and return disappointed, and he felt sad for that. He didn't understand how to start a conversation, what to talk about, and how much to talk about. That's how his personality was. Whatever he would tell people, no matter how much, they wouldn't know that all he had talked about was a lie. Still, it was difficult for him. It didn't work.

But there was one smiling face looking at him, often doing it every week she visited the place. He, too, replied with a smile automatically and did not resist the smile. She used to visit with her parents and he came every evening to sit here, just for her. The five-year-old girl, he wouldn't know what she looked for, in him. Her parents told Nihit that she does not let anyone come near her but him. She even starts crying and screaming, they said. Her father treated Nihit like his younger brother, and Nihit, he didn't know how did he treat that little angel.

He would always have a chocolate for her every time she visited. Innocently she used to reach to his pocket for that chocolate.

A month or two flew so early. He had brought it that day

also. But she was not there. She did not visit there anymore. After passing another month, she still didn't arrive, and neither did her parents. Nihit did not try to find her. The chocolates remained in his pocket every day he visited. But he did not give it to any other child visited with their parents. He didn't like to share her chocolates with someone else.

A Play

After another hour's ride, they reached the cemetery. Leaves were scattered everywhere. Kayra knew this particular cemetery and the town they had just left behind. This was where she had lost someone important, to the point that she wasn't ready to leave the town, hoping he would be back one day.

Now that Nihit had brought her to this place, she wasn't puzzled. Her heartbeats were faster than ever as she walked behind him. He stopped at a particular tomb and put the flowers he bought for his mother near the coffee shop. Nihit had too many things to talk about with his mother. He wanted to tell her that he missed her, almost every day! He wanted to ask if she was doing alright this whole time when her son was away. He sat beside and moved his hand slowly over the tomb.

Kayra, on the other hand, had turmoil in her heart to know all this. She did not know how to react. To express sympathy watching him in pain, to be angry that he left her in the middle of nowhere, or to show happiness that he was back in her life after all these years.

"Mother, you remember her?" he looked at Kayra.

She knelt beside him, already with tears in her eyes. Out of words, she just looked at him. Nihit reached out to hold her hand, but she refused to cooperate, pushed him and ran out of the cemetery. But he sat there leaning his back to the vertical member of the tomb, took out the mouth organ, and sat still. He did not play it. That was one of the two treasures he had.

After some time, when he was back at the cemetery gate, Kayra was sitting on the bench. Still, tears rolling down her eyes. A few strands of hairs stick to her face. Nihit reached out and slowly wiped her eyes. She didn't say a word, and neither did he!

"How could you do this?" She asked after a few more seconds and waited for the answer. He didn't answer. "Say something, damn it! Answer me!" she punched him on his chest, and he didn't retreat. He pulled her and took her in his embrace. She became hostile again. "All these years, where the hell were you? I loved you! And you left me just like that! Didn't even bother to contact me once, at least! Why would you come now?" He still didn't answer. His hand reached out to hers, and he realized she is clutching something in her fist. But as he held her wrist, she loosened the grip. The ring! His second treasure was safe. She threw herself in his arms and cried out, clutching him for a long time. He rubbed her head slowly, trying to coax her. She tightened her embrace each second rubbing her face against his chest.

"Okay, now let's go." He said a few moments later.

"No!" she replied childishly, with no intention to let him go anywhere this time. He let her hug him and snuggle. When they drove back to the café, it was dark already. In the café, she sat holding his arm, leaning her head over his shoulder.

Just after their order arrived, Nihit's cell rang. It was Jay. Before he could say anything, a voice fell on his ear, "Nihit, Gayatri did not reach home."

"What do you mean by that?"

"I have confirmed from her office colleagues that she left

her office half an hour ago but did not reach the home, and her cell is off."

"Okay, I'll do something." Nihit assured him.

When Nihit was about to call a number, the exact number popped up. "Boss, your sister is in danger. I've been following them. They are headed to the outskirts of the city." The other party provided the information. Fortunately, Nihit was already out of the city; it could take another ten or fifteen minutes to reach the place he was referring to.

The next thing Nihit did was to call Karan and ask him to pick up and drop Kayra at her hostel. Kayra was puzzled by these two-three constant calls and could see the changes in expressions on Nihit's face.

"I've to go. Karan will pick you up. Take care of yourself." he said, kissed her forehead, and sat in the car.

"But..." Kayra wanted to say something.

"I'll tell you later," he had no time.

The engine roared, and the car sped away. Nihit turned the vehicle towards the cemetery again. Behind the cemetery was a road from the forest to the city's outskirts. He was getting anxious more and more. He made another call and asked for the location. "I'm not sure, but I can't catch them. They're fast. You know the abandoned area near the Brooklet; I think that's where they are headed." The other party provided some more information.

In ten minutes, his car crossed the bridge over the Brooklet and in another ten minutes, his car reached the area of abandoned houses. As he stepped out of the car, he could see a white car, an old model of Fiat, parked in front of one of the houses. There was nothing except the car. But if there was a car, there must be someone at least. The guess was correct. He rushed towards one of the houses.

A person was standing at the door, with a knife in his hand, playing with it. Inside the room, two had removed Gayatri's tied hands. She was unconscious all the way. They had used chloroform when she was at the stop she usually waited for the cab. When no one was around, they made her fall unconscious and tied her hands.

They were careless in their job. They didn't cover her mouth. Because even if she awakened, her hands were tied, and if she screamed, the window glasses were closed; plus, it was the moving van, so, no one would have bothered, no one would have noticed. After reaching the place, even if she shouted or struggled, there was no use. The place where she was waiting for her cab was not the place they could kill someone, so they kidnapped her first. Initially, they just kidnapped her to kill her, but their dirty minds had something else now, after kidnapping her. The girl was beautiful, and they did not want to waste it.

As Gayatri returned to her senses, she was scared to see the strangers. Besides, she was lying on the bed. As soon as they noticed she was awake, one of the two said, "Don't be surprised. You're our guest for today!" and laughed out.

Gayatri instantly leaped to the door but was blocked by the second guy and was pushed back on the bed again. "Well, whatever you try, will be useless."

"Look, let me go, spare me please, what I've done to you?"

"Nothing, but we want something out of you, with your permission or without."

A cold sweat gathered on Gayatri's forehead. She was

scared and soon realized what they had in their dirty minds, but looking at the situation, she concluded that there was no way out. She wanted to die before anything or anyone could harm her dignity. She had tears in her eyes, "Please, let me go."

"Who the hell are you? What are…" Before the person on the watch could complete, he cried, "Ah…" Nihit had suddenly attacked the goon, and the knife slipped and fell to the ground. Nihit bent, lifted the blade, and stabbed the thigh of the goon who was on the watch. Inside, the two were stunned to hear a cry; it was their partner's voice. Before the goon could react, Nihit reached out and gave a sharp cut on his hand too. Nihit grabbed him and smashed his head against the wall. The goon fainted and fell to the floor. Nihit kicked the door, and with a bang, the door was open to the inside.

His face turned pale, and his eyes darkened with killing intents. One of the two attacked and threw a punch at Nihit's face, but he dodged the attack and grabbed the fist. The guy couldn't move his hand, he felt like his hand was trapped in a giant steel clamp. Nihit straightened his arm and threw a solid punch to his stomach. To the goon's dismay, he couldn't even calculate the speed; keep the thought of dodging it away. The goon buckled onto his knees. Nihit lifted his right leg, and his knee banged on the goon's lower jaw, breaking his teeth. The goon groaned in pain. Nihit left him in the same condition, suddenly turned, and his right leg flew in the air, landing on the chest of the other goon. The person flew back and landed on the open window's sharp edge. He spat out a mouthful of blood and fainted on the spot.

Gayatri ran and threw herself in Nihit's arms, crying. She

clutched him tightly, "They, they wanted to..." she sobbed continuously. Nihit put his left arm around her and rubbed her hair with his right, trying to calm her, "Sshhh... It's okay, don't worry. I'm here!" They walked out of the house. Gayatri was still in his embrace, neither he let go of her for a long time. "I'm here. No one can harm you anymore." He gently stroked Gayatri's head.

In less than another ten minutes or so, two cars stopped making screeching noises. Jay and a handsome guy stepped out of the car and walked towards Nihit. From another car, Karan rushed to them; he was panicked too.

As soon as the handsome guy faced Nihit, Nihit gestured something; the guy nodded and headed to the house.

"Gayatri, go home with Jay." Nihit talked to Gayatri, who was still in his embrace.

"Brother..."

"I'll be back soon, love. Just behind you, okay." he assured her.

He looked into Jay's eyes and gestured something. Gayatri walked to the car with Jay, and both left. After asking about Kayra, Nihit also sent Karan back. After that, he turned to the house. The handsome guy had already dragged the person lying on the door inside.

The window was open, and the moonlight could reach the room's floor. Nihit sat on the chair, leaning forward. In front of him, all three were lying unconscious. Nihit looked at the handsome guy, and he threw a bucket of water at them. Slowly all returned to their senses and suddenly, a crisp voice echoed in the room—slap to the one at the door.

"Speak." Nihit's voice was authoritative as he lightened

                                    The Whistler

a cigarette.

Suddenly all three stood up to leap on Nihit.

"Hey, hey, watch it, boys," the handsome guy had a gun pointed toward them.

"I don't like to repeat," Nihit's voice was calm, yet cold.

"Are you looking for a death?" The goon replied arrogantly.

As soon as the question was completed, Nihit flicked a cigarette and waved his elbow that landed on the chest of the goon, who was arrogant just now, making the goon cough badly. The moment he buckled, his knee landed on his jaw. The moment he was straight, a fist hit the chest and he fell to the ground with a loud thud on his back. Nihit walked to him, squeezed the goon's right arm under his left shoe, and the goon screamed hysterically. Then suddenly, a kick landed on the goon's lower jaw, and there was a neck-breaking noise. Nihit jumped, pointing his knee to the goon's chest. There was a thud, the movement of the goon's right hand struggling to the ground, and no activity. The forceful blow landed directly on the heart, stopping it and causing death on the spot.

The remaining two goons froze to death, no one dared to move an inch, and their legs started shaking. They were terrified. The other party could kill a person, only in a few moves in a minute, that too, without a weapon. They had understood there was no escape from this monster standing before them. They had committed the mistake of messing with the girl. Their faces turned pale with fear. A stream of sweat rolled down through a forehead to the cheeks of the second goon as Nihit walked behind him.

"Speak!" Nihit lit another cigarette.

"We, we don't know anything." the second one replied.

The goon knelt on the ground as Nihit hit his left leg. Out of nowhere, a blade slid into his hand, he turned it around, and the wooden floor was bloody only in a few seconds, and the goon was dead, writhing in pain, his body twitching for a minute or so. Watching the blood flowing underneath his legs, the last goon nearly fainted but did not fall unconscious. He looked miserable.

"Speak."

"We received the orders from our boss. I know nothing else than this. We kidnapped her, and Sameer, the one who died first, came up with this dirty idea that..." he didn't dare to complete the sentence.

"Name your boss?"

"Vijay from the black valley of..." the moment his name came out of his throat, there was a gunshot between his eyes. Another three gunshots echoed in the city's outskirts, where no one could hear the sound.

Nihit bent a little and picked up the mouth organ which has fallen from his pocket while he was fighting. The blood dribbled from the corner of it. Drip! Drip! Drip! A smile appeared on Nihit's corners of his lips as he left the room while blowing a whistle.

The black beauty's engine roared and the handsome guy drove Nihit to his home and left to complete the business. Jay's heart skipped a bit as he noticed the blood on Nihit's sleeve. The coldness in his eyes still hasn't vanished. "Did she eat?" he asked Jay.

Jay shook his head no and asked him, "What did you

do?"

"Nothing, just some necessary thing," Nihit's voice was merely a hoarse. After washing up, Nihit went to the kitchen and made Gayatri's favorite food. That took around twenty minutes, and he carried a plate to her bed. She was sitting like a frightened little kitten, totally messed up.

He slowly walked to her and placed the plate on the table near the bed. Pulled Gayatri and made her sit properly. She hasn't said a word since she returned home. She even refused to eat when Jay offered her, and Jay didn't force her.

Nihit fed her the meal, and she ate it obediently. Then Gayatri slept on his lap, clutching his hand. He rubbed her hair gently and sat the whole night without sleep in his eyes while Gayatri slept in harmony. Her brother had promised her that no one will harm her anymore!

The Stories Around

In the abandoned area to the East of the city Vizag, a few of the houses were in a condition that they could be used. The houses were of wooden material. A few years back they were used as warehouses for businesses. As for the time being, they were not in good condition because of termites and rain, but the place was perfect for a person like him and his motive.

The door was closed. Inside the house, a person sat leaning his back on the chair facing the wall. A photo of the person on the wall had an arrow on his face. A few more pictures stick to the wall in which the boy was younger than now. The photos could show all the phases from sixteen to twenty-five. A few years were missing, though, because the person in the pictures was untraceable in those years. The person in the photographs looked handsome, wearing a cream-colored frame on his eyes. The person had a lean body and had the same sense of clothes in almost all the photos.

Sachin sat there staring at the photos for almost an hour. His eyes were showing rage, which could burn someone alive. The person in the photograph had made Sachin lose his life and now, there was only one target in his life: the person's death in the pictures.

The first time he made a move were ten years ago, at night, sending a few boys by giving them some money. Sachin wanted that person to get beaten so that he looks like dead. The person will lose all of his strength, and Sachin will come into the action. Instead, they were beaten back. Sachin could have killed him already, in his town. But when he tried, the person survived, and his mother died in the accident. Before he could try again, the person had flown out of the town. Just vanished, yet Sachin had discovered that person again in Vizag.

The next move Sachin planned when he called out those boys again. But this time, Sachin saw a girl with that person. Who might that be? After watching him fight the boys who tried to bully that girl, Sachin didn't want to kill him. Before killing him, the person needed to feel the pain of loss. I have my target, for now, Sachin thought, leaving the boys fighting with him.

Sachin planned to meet those boys again to make a deal and let the person bear the pain of loss by killing his sister. For the time being, she was the most important person and the closest one to him. But the next day, the newspaper had the story of two people getting shot dead, and Sachin could not find those boys again. Whatever he did or planned, he just ultimately wanted to hurt the person in the photograph. But in the next few months, the person left the city, leaving his sister behind. Sachin did not want to do it behind his back. He should be there. The person needs to watch it with his own eyes. The greater the involvement of emotions, the greater the pain!

Sachin did let it go for the time being! Whether he let it go or not, he has to chase the person throughout. But Sachin had lost his trail, and the person was in the wind. Sachin could not find the person for years. Like this, Sachin could not hurt him. It would have been better if he had killed the person already as Sachin had many chances, but he didn't act. He waited for the right time.

Years later, Sachin found the person again in Vizag.

Sachin did not know where the person was or what he had done in those years. All he knew was that he had found another chance, and now, Sachin could not lose him again. He could not allow this to happen. There wasn't any slightest chance for that. Sachin stalked him, followed him wherever he went and whatever he did. Then he watched him grow with the business. Each time he looked at the photograph, whatever he had forgotten would flash in front of his eyes, and his mind would be filled with all the things that happened a decade ago, which made his life miserable and even worse. But he had to bear that, and he did.

After waiting for a decade, Sachin was now sure that he could make his move. The person in the photograph was back to his sister. This was the perfect time to kill his sister. Plus, there was someone else too, whom he loved and snatching the most beloved people from his life would destroy the person to the ground. As same as what happened to him a decade ago!

Sachin sat for some more time and left the room.

At the table, far from where he was sitting, three men sat discussing their lady boss, how her behavior and looks were precisely opposite. From their talk, it was clear that she was charming, and her boobs had a nice size. Though, she was a workaholic and didn't entertain any of the bullshit they were trying. But they hoped, someday, it would happen what they wanted.

On the table behind Sachin, two young men sat discussing the girl one of them loved. He didn't turn, but the conversation was about how the girl had left one of them miserable—another story of someone's broken heart and why they were having drinks.

On the table next to him sat four people. The young one in his early twenties held a cigarette in his hand and the wine placed before him. The middle-aged person tried to convince him to stop smoking; it kills, as smoke directly attacks the lungs. At the same time, the young one refuted that the wine also directly attacks the liver. And the answer made a middle-aged man look like nonsense. But the middle-aged man again said it takes much longer than a cigarette. That's the same! Slow death! The young one replied with pain in his eyes, thinking that the day his parents say that their son is capable of something, of anything, he would not touch it. The other two watched the heated argument and tried to ease the atmosphere at the table, blabbering some more nonsense, and later, they enjoyed their wine.

Sachin was sitting in the Zero Degree bar at a distance of not less than 500 meters and not more than 600 meters from his wooden house. After 8 pm, a person walked into the bar and sat at the table before Sachin. Sachin ordered the wine for himself and the person who had just arrived. They had their drinks, and both walked to the wooden house. The bearded guy from the bar also followed them both. It was dark outside.

They reached into Sachin's room, and Sachin sat on the chair, maintaining his calm composure. "What the hell were you thinking?" After sitting for a minute or so, Sachin demanded the answer from the goon.

"I just ordered them to kill her. I don't know what went

wrong," the other person replied and had fear in his voice, "give me another chance. This time she won't survive." The person tried to explain things to Sachin. It was regular for them to kidnap someone for ransom or kill if the money was enough. The person wouldn't be afraid of things like this usually. But while standing before Sachin, there was something in his mind at that particular moment that could be called a terror.

"There is no next time," Sachin rose from the chair suddenly. And the person next to him felt something on his stomach. He felt pain. He touched it, and his hand became red. The red fluid made him feel horrified. He looked at Sachin holding the knife, and knelt on the ground, holding and pressing his stomach, trying to stop the blood flow. His agony was unbearable; his mind was filled with the only thing, death. Sachin bent a little, playing with the blood-red knife in his hand. "Did you think this is just another case of killing someone? It seems it wasn't!" Sachin's eyes and intense voice made the perfect combination to frighten anyone.

"Let me go, spare me this one time. I'll do anything you want," the person pleaded with a gasp in his broken voice. There was no strength in him to scream; even if he did, no one would have heard it. The bearded person just watched everything in silence.

"You had one job! I gave you enough money to do it, and you failed me." Sachin was still calm. The goon was even more horrified to see the person doing such things with such calmness. "I paid you to kill her! Not to play with the girl," he took a pause, "plus, I don't like that part of the story, ever!"

                                        The Whistler

as he completed his sentence, the goon made some more noise, but not enough. The noise could not even reach out of that abandoned house. Sachin watched the knife dribbling the blood to the ground he had just removed from the goon's neck and threw it on the floor.

Sachin walked out of the house, set it on fire, and threw out the skinned gloves. Afterward, he walked in the dark on the raw path behind the bar towards the valley. There was a single streetlight in the dark and a blazing fire behind him. But that didn't scare Sachin; there was nothing he would be scared of. Not anymore! He blew a whistle while walking into the dark.

The newspaper next day said that till someone noticed the fire and reported it to the fire brigade; all they could find was the ash and a corp. Even his face could not be identified! The person was burned to death, and the smoke might have killed him. But the forensic report of the police investigation had something interesting to say: the person they found was dead already before the fire.

Sachin had destroyed the evidences that could lead anyone to him. Moreover, he didn't need to do it; no one knew him by the name he used. Even if someone came up to him, there was no evidence against him. Nevertheless, he used this name for a purpose. He wanted someone to know this, only a particular person. With this name, as a Sachin Dixit, only one person could recognize him, Nihit. All the misfortune and dreadful things happened in Nihit's life; this name was the reason!

Now that he failed, Sachin had learned that the enemy

was not weak and also was with the sources. Not only could Nihit reach the spot on time for his sister, but he killed the goons mercilessly. As for the cops, they even could not think who might have done this stuff. Nihit not only cares for those he loves but also has their back; he doesn't want them to get hurt. That became the most thrilling challenge for Sachin because it would give his enemy the pain he wanted to give. Sachin, himself was going to do this now. And this was going to satisfy him more than anything…

A Silent Warning

After leaving Kayra with Karan at the cafe that evening, the next day after college hours, Nihit didn't show up to meet her. She tried to reach him, but his number wasn't reachable. She felt depressed subconsciously.

After waiting a few more minutes at their daily spot when she thought he wouldn't arrive, she was on the way back to her hostel. Just walking a few steps, she heard a bike roar behind her. As she was about to turn, something hit her back of the head; she felt a sharp pain; the bike hit her, and she fell to the ground. The motorcycle stopped a few meters away, the biker with the helmet made more noise hitting the accelerator, and the bike disappeared.

Kayra tried to crumple and stood. She felt something warm on her left cheek, and the pain on her forehead made her realize the wound on her forehead. She touched her cheek, and as she looked at her bloody hand, she fell unconscious.

When she slowly opened her eyes, she was lying on the bed until past eleven at night. She tried to figure out the place, moved her eyes around, and found Nihit sitting on the table beside her. "Hey, you're awake!" his voice had concern. He reached out to help her to sit. "How are you feeling now?"

"My head is aching." Kayra made a face. She touched her forehead and found it covered with the round bandage. "You still look like a princess!" said Nihit, realizing she noticed the bandage around her head. Her lips curled into a sweet smile. He reached out and stroked her hair gently. "Hungry?" he asked; she shook her head yes. Then he fed her the meal himself. "You'll be alright!" he assured her. "Take some rest." He said and let her sleep again after she was full. He sat beside her and stroked her head; she fell asleep shortly; she was exhausted.

Nihit switched off the lights and was about to leave. But a gush of wind came through, and he realized the window was open. The moonlight from the window fell on Kayra's face, and he sat a few more minutes watching the sleeping innocence. The wind flew her hair and covered her half face. She was still wearing a casual shirt and knee-length skirt as she thought he loved to see her this way.

After some time, he came out of the hospital to smoke. He walked to the backside of the hospital. There was a narrow raw path facing the forest. The last golden-colored street lamp was glowing at a distance of around 50 meters. Everything after the light was dark, and a few rays were scattered through the branches and leaves of the trees. He walked beneath one of such large trees and lightened his cigarette. The dry leaves made some noise in the eerie silence as his feet crushed them.

All the time, his mind was throbbing. Something's wrong; this can't be a coincidence. There's someone behind this. There must be. Someone followed him a month back whenever he visited the college; he could sense it for almost half of a month. And then, suddenly, he couldn't feel it anymore. The person had backed off. Could it be that he got whatever he wanted? The one who had taken the contract to kidnap Gayatri, Vijay from some black valley was murdered anonymously. Nihit knew that from his sources. As for those who made the mistake of touching Gayatri, Nihit himself had silenced them. But the master was still out there who was giving the orders, who had hired Vijay. It was apparent that the person who hired Vijay, only he was responsible for Vijay's death. He was still out there...

In less than five minutes, a shadow appeared in front of Nihit, but a person could not be found, just a shadow of someone. "Boss, I've my eyes on those we thought would be troublesome." The shadow took a pause, "This seems a new one. I'll find out soon but need some time." Nihit nodded, and the shadow disappeared shortly. Nihit didn't have time, the two most important people he loved were attacked in two days, and he could not sit quietly but had no other choice.

The next day Karan came over to look out for Kayra. "Watch out for yourself. You should be careful. How are you now, by the way?" Karan said, looking at Kayra with concern in his voice. As for the time being, only he knew about her. She was yet to be introduced to Nihit's family.

"I'll take a note of that." She responded, making an apologetic face. She was getting discharged from the hospital as injuries were minimal, and she could take care of it herself. 'Moreover, Nihit is there', Kayra thought to herself. The bandage was still there, around her head. While Kayra and Nihit noted what the doctor was telling, Karan helped them with the formalities. After carefully listening to the doctor's advice and precautions, both walked out of the hospital.

Outside the hospital, Karan spoke to someone on a call and said, "Nihit, a friend of mine was passing by, and he is in the city, he wants to meet you, for the business co-operation. I hope you won't mind meeting him once." He looked at Nihit with nervousness.

"Sure!" Nihit replied casually with a smile. Karan was a good friend and had helped him in many things. Even he was there this time to ask about Kayra's wellness. Nihit could meet that person happily. Nihit opened the door for Kayra and closed it after she got in. He got into the driver's seat, and the black beauty sped into the city.

As the car was getting away, a figure stood there, with fire in his eyes, till the vehicle blurred and vanished eventually. The figure thought, *'It's the time. The play begins now..!*

The Whistle

Kayra wasn't home when Nihit reached. As his phone buzzed, her name appeared on the screen. It was a text from Kayra. She had asked him to arrive at the Seminary Hills. He walked out of the house to the car in his garage and sat on the driver's seat. As he ignited the engine, the cell chimed again with another call, showing the unknown number. He pressed the receive button, and before he could speak, a voice fell on his ear, "Hi there! I'll be killing a nice girl today, and I happen to know that you care for her. Well, I don't want to, she is nice, a nice person I envy, but I will anyway. Also, I don't have to, if you stop me, of course, which you can't!" the person seemed to be smiling while talking, and Nihit could sense that the person was enjoying, "well, if you can't, at least you can try. Don't say I didn't warn you; save her if you can!"

Nihit knew what the other party meant and whom it was referring to. He instantly called Kayra to inform her, but there was no answer. He then called another number, said a few things, slipped his mobile into the pocket and shifted the reverse gear; the tires made the screeching noise. As the car turned onto the main road, he pressed the accelerator pedal with all his might and force, shifting the forward gears.

A car reached the place, Seminary Hills. The place was crowded with people. He parked his car in a hurry, stepped out, and saw Kayra's scooty parked. Indeed, she was already there, waiting. He was praying and hoping that someone might not hurt her in a crowded place like that.

Nihit rushed to the crowded area and found her sitting on the bench. She rose from the bench as she saw him from a distance. He ran to her with anxiety. She just walked a few steps and felt something sharp on her neck. She knelt on the ground in no time. "Kayra…" Nihit screamed and ran to her. His face turned pale; he was afraid; he was in despair, had eyes full of tears; he knelt before her. He held her in his arms helplessly. Her lips opened to say something and trembled but couldn't complete anything, and then, she was no more.

He held her hugging, his shirt stained with the blood. He sat calling her name a few more times. People looked in the direction of the scream and gathered around murmuring. The young person was holding a beautiful girl.

"What is happening here? Why did he scream?"

"Wait a minute! Is that blood on her neck? Is she dead?"

At a distance, out of the crowd, a figure stood unnoticed by everyone, observing everything with cold eyes. Putting his left hand in his pocket, and another playing with a cigarette. As he crushed the filter, he turned and left while blowing the whistle.

The Survival

Seven cops were dealing with the murder case in less than an hour. Inspector Das was a man of thirty-nine. He moved to the dead body of a girl. *'The cut has more impact on the left and less on the right.'* He thought and turned his neck to the left. He watched as far as he could, counted something in his mind, and walked. An old Fiat was parked no less than 50 meters in the trees. After observing, it was clear that it was abandoned, but the handle had no dust like other places over the car. Someone just used the door handle, the inspector thought. He opened the door with a handkerchief, and obviously, it was clear someone had used the car to sit there.

While Kayra's body had been sent for the postmortem, people were getting interrogated after a few hours. A table was placed in the middle of the room and two people sat opposite to each other. The hanging lamp could focus only on half of the face of both persons, while the remaining area of the room was dark. One had a calm face, but his eyes could tell the pain; he was getting interrogated. The other one looked agitated, but you could not say if he was or not; he was the inspector.

"Mr. Jay, I am sorry for your loss." Inspector Das said with sympathy. "How did this happen?"

"I don't know. I was late." Jay replied.

"How do you know her?" the inspector asked

"Kayra. She is a friend. I know her through Nihit. They were together."

The inspector paused for few seconds and asked, "Who

is Nihit?"

"Nihit Naik is my friend and a brother!"

The Inspector twitched his eyes and looked doubtful. "Why would someone want to kill her? Do you suspect anyone?"

"No." Jay looked agitated now. For sure, he too wanted to know. "I don't know," Jay replied sincerely. Yet, he thought.

"When did you meet her last time?"

"Today in the morning, before I left for the office." Jay said.

"Noticed anything abnormal about her recently?"

"Not really." Jay replied.

'That's a lie!' The inspector thought.

"Does her death affects you?"

"Yes, because it affects Nihit. I can't see him miserable and deceived." There was pain in his voice for his brother.

"How do you know Nihit? I mean, he is not your brother by blood, right?" the inspector asked, raising his brows. It seemed that before interrogation, the inspector had done his homework.

"I met him eleven years back. One morning I was on the morning walk and found him under a tree, shivering because of the rain. And we stayed together."

"You trusted him?" the inspector asked, narrowing his eyes.

"No. Not in the beginning. But he gained that trust." Jay answered without even blinking and counter-questioned, "Do you have your parents, inspector?"

The inspector looked at Jay with questioning eyes.

"Here's the thing with us orphans," Jay answered to that look, "First of all, in some cases, they survive themselves. Second, the luckier meet good people. Third, they fall into the wrong hands, and you might know what they do."

"Why are you telling me this?" the inspector wasn't agitated anymore. The person sitting before him was talking sensibly.

"I'm just coming to that," Jay explained further, "I fall into the first category, and we orphans need allies. How do you think we survive, inspector?" Jay's question was reasonable.

'No fear at all!' The inspector thought.

In the middle of an interrogation, Jay remembered the night when he was sixteen.

* * *

At around four in the early morning, Jay sneaked out of his room. There was no sleep in his eyes since he knew Nihit fought with the boys who tried to bully him and Gayatri. He didn't ask them but knew it anyway. He slightly pushed the door of Nihit's room, found Gayatri sitting at the head of Nihit, and was asleep. Nihit was having nightmares that night; that's why Gayatri was there. Jay turned around and stepped out of the house.

The night was scary. The lightning and the heavy rain made it difficult to watch everything that could be in front of anyone. But he had to do it. He tightened the grip around the gun he had in his hand and walked towards the new seven-storied construction building.

The fire was visible on the ground floor from a distance. Three figures sat around discussing something important to them, making a circle around the fire. Jay reached, gathering all his courage. He stopped a few meters away, and they saw him with a gun after the lightning. It was shocking for them to see someone with a gun at this age. They asked him who he was and what he was doing at this hour, but he didn't seem to bother about that. All the sleeping figures were awake with sleepy eyes. Before they could understand anything, there was a big sound. And the sound repeated twice.

All he did was point his gun suddenly and shoot two adults. The boys were horrified to look at him. The blood splashed around the ground and on the walls froze them to death. No one dared to move an inch.

Jay threatened them to leave the town as soon as possible instead of killing them. They had considered themselves dead already. But they sighed out of relief when the person gave them another chance to live and leave. The boys had seen him with Nihit a few days before and knew why he would kill their masters! But they were scared and not in a state to say anything. They were alive! That was enough for them.

Jay turned to return and stopped suddenly; the boys panicked again. But he only stood and fired a shot in the soil and let his gun drop the rain through his gunpoint to the ground. He left the site shortly and sneaked into his house. He once again made sure that Gayatri and Nihit were asleep. He smiled and went back to his room.

"Alright..! How did you reach over there?" the inspector asked his next question, and Jay returned to the reality.

"I was called out." He replied.

"By whom?"

"Nihit. He called me to reach for her. He was on the way. He asked me if I could accompany her till he gets there."

"You can go." The inspector said. Jay reached to the door. "And..." inspector was about to say something...

"And I request you not to leave the town, and if you remember anything that could help to get this criminal behind bars, you can contact me," Jay completed the line for the inspector while walking out of the door.

The Inspector smiled wickedly, "I'd appreciate that."

Shortly after that, another person was sitting at the place where Jay sat a few minutes back. His eyes were red under the frame, and they had cold expressions. The person looked defeated and had suffered an enormous loss. He looked calm, but the inspector could see that he was not. His shirt was still red with the blood.

"Mr. Nihit, I feel sorry for your loss."

"No. You don't!" Nihit snapped back.

"Well, that's what we have to say the least," the inspector said, trying to cover the situation. "How do you know Kayra?" inspector's next question was ready.

"I, I loved her!" His voice had a void.

Life Happens

He sat beside his mother's tomb for a long time after burying his mother. Everyone had returned and he only sat there. His friend let him stay with his mother for a while. But even after the dark, when he did not return, Kayra was worried for him. After waiting for some more time, she decided to find him and reached the cemetery only to find him asleep next to his mother's tomb, spreading his arms over it. She touched him by his shoulder, and he woke up slowly. She looked into his eyes; even in the dark, she could tell that they were red.

"Nihit..., what are you doing here?" She asked him hesitantly, "Let's go home."

He looked into zero, "Home? But the mother is here!" His eyes were looking for something, and his voice had a void. Perhaps they were looking for a home, for his mother.

She had no answer to that and kept silent. She stayed with him, sitting beside him as long as he was there. She wanted to comfort him, say something, or give him a warm hug, but she didn't.

Seven months ago, Nihit sat trying to play the mouth organ his mother bought him. He tried to learn this new instrument his mother gave him on his birthday just a week before. The more he wanted to play it, the more it frustrated him. When he blew the air, it would sound, it would sound even after sucking the air, and that made it more difficult for him.

While he was trying, a car arrived slowly and stopped a block away. A lady of his mother's age stepped out of the car and followed by the lady, a beautiful angel climbed down from the car holding a book. She stood a few moments patiently, and once her mother gave her a box, she placed the book on the box and grabbed the box. Her mother went inside with the luggage bag, and the beauty struggled to move the curly strand of hair falling on her face with a jerk, which annoyed her. As she was struggling, Nihit had already reached out to her. Without thinking twice, he slowly tucked that strand behind her ear to help her out...

The angel blinked several times, looking at the boy who had a smile on his face and wore glasses on his eyes. She let him do what he was doing and didn't say anything. She was mature enough, and his behavior made her think of the innocence the boy next to her had. He had the mouth organ in his left hand. She wondered if the boy before her could play it nicely. And her lips broke into a slow smile!

Kayra's mother walked out of the door with a smile on her face watching this innocent act of the boy. But the next moment, Nihit's mother arrived, and the ladies seemed to know each other. There was a formal introduction, and the ladies walked inside the house talking about something. But Nihit didn't bother to hear what they were talking about.

Nihit was fourteen, and Kayra was a year older than him. The house where Kayra and her mother had shifted was empty for more than six months as the old owner had sold it and moved to the city with his son. Kayra's mother has been a single mother since her father died in the accident a couple of years back.

Days flew with the speed of the wind, and both came closer and closer. While his parents argued without even realizing that their son was watching them, Nihit would walk to the Brooklet near the house and sit there, watching the water flow, trying to ignore everything around him.

But now, there was someone else too, with him. Kayra would be there whenever he visited the Brooklet bank and sat on the rock. The angel would blink her eyes, making him forget his sorrow of pain. She would tell him the stories where there would be a boy and a girl. Almost every tale had a happy ending, unlike his parents. Whenever Kayra mentioned anything about the girl, Nihit would stare at her. "What?!" she would ask him tapping his forehead, and he would shake his head at nothing and turn his eyes. He wouldn't talk much, and she never complained about it. Kayra would hold his hand and roam with him near the Brooklet. She would tell him that she would marry him once he was twenty-one. Listening to that, his smile would widen. "Oh my!" She would laugh wholeheartedly, watching him blushing. Nevertheless, she didn't lie about her wish to marry him.

While his parents didn't give him attention, Kayra was his only escape from everything. There were a few friends, but he would go to them occasionally. The teen love was blossoming anonymous to everyone. He would forget his pain and be the happiest person ever with her. Five months flew by, and they did not even realize that.

In the following months, his parents separated, and he lived with his mother. And just after a month, his mother died in a car accident. The same night Nihit left the town. There was no sign of him when Kayra woke up at the tomb. She felt something in her palm; it was the ring. She recognized it was from Nihit's mother; she gave it to him in her last moments. Kayra ran to her mother, "Mother, where is Nihit?"

"What happened, beta? You were with him. And why are you panting?" Her mother asked with concern.

"Mother, when I woke up, he wasn't there." Kayra had water in her eyes already, on the verge of crying.

"What do you mean by he wasn't there?"

When it was too dark in the early morning, Nihit left. They tried to find out wherever they could. They enquired to his father, but he didn't visit him either. He was gone! The group of boys Nihit hanged out a few times was dead just a couple of days before, which shook Kayra and her mother to the core.

***

"When did you meet her?" The inspector continued his interrogation.

"A few months back, in her college." Nihit replied.

"Where were you at the time of the murder?"

"I don't remember where exactly I was. I was on the way to meet her." Nihit looked straight into the inspector's eyes. If it were not for inspector Das and another person, he would have been terrified of that look.

What is it you trying to hide, the inspector thought, and he was sure about it.

"Do you suspect anyone?" inspector took a pause, "Why would someone want to kill her?"

"I don't know." Nihit replied.

After some more questions, Nihit walked out of the interrogation room, as the inspector did not want to bother the person who had just lost his loved one and looked utterly messed up. It was their job to find out who the killer was. Also, Nihit could not provide any detail that could help them. Nonetheless, he wouldn't tell them even if he knew. He, himself wanted to kill the murderer.

Karan sat outside the college canteen, late in the afternoon, thinking about what the inspector would ask him. Since the inspector wanted to meet him, he was nervous. Though, he wasn't called out at the station. The inspector said he was headed somewhere and wanted just a few minutes of talk.

"Mr. Karan, I apologize to bother you, but we are doing our job." Inspector Das asked him, "How do you know Nihit?"

"A few months back Jay introduced us in the college."

"How do you know Kayra?"

"I barely know anything about her. Just know formal things. Except for her name and relationship with Nihit, I only know that she was a bright student. That's all."

"How were the things between Kayra and Nihit?"

"Just like any other normal couple out there. You shouldn't suspect them. Besides, it's useless. He loved her, and she loved him back!"

"Do you know or think that Kayra had an enemy who could hurt her?"

"I don't know, inspector."

"What about Nihit?"

"Not sure, but there is a possibility that he might have some..." Karan said hesitantly.

"Why would that be?"

"He runs a business. There might be rivals or so. Just frankly, I'm not sure about it either."

"Alight. I'll take a leave then. Please let me know if you remember anything that can help us."

"For sure," Karan replied, and the inspector left..

A Rich Bird

Kirti sat on the sofa in her house, sipping the coffee. She had let her long hair open. She didn't remember the last time her beautiful long hair flew in the air. She could have an excellent life partner if she were an ordinary girl with normal ambitions. But she was not. She sat watching the repeated telecast of the news, where reporters were asking inspector Das questions about serial murders in the city; citizens were frightened as they were not safe. There might be a psycho on the roads or someone much more dangerous than that, and the police department could not do anything about it. Inspector Das was telling that they are doing their best in the investigating to put the criminals behind the bars.

As for the murders, Kirti had already realized that the dead were goons. Not a single person out of them was innocent, except a girl named Kayra!

Inspector Das reached Kirti's house, and she could see the worried face of the inspector. She invited inspector Das in and offered him a cup of coffee.

"Too much confusion…!" said inspector Das and sat next to Kirti, "Months earlier, there were three murders on the outskirts of the city. One died because his heart had stopped forcefully. He had injuries too; even his neck was broken. The other one had his throat sliced, and before death, the broken bones. The third one had a bullet between the eyes." The inspector sighed helplessly. "Who can kill someone with such kind of rage? And there are these, another three, with the same fate. The pattern is same."

"And what about the girl?" Kirti looked at him with

questioning eyes.

"She was murdered in a broad daylight, in the crowd itself!"

"What do we have on that case?"

"Nothing yet..!" he replied.

"Well, then get me everything on her boyfriend, Nihit!" Kirti said thoroughly. She already had something in her mind.

The next day in the police station, inspector Das was ready with all the details he was asked for. "Why would you ask about him? The poor fellow... So far, he has lost the love of his life." Inspector Das said with pity. "What's so interesting about him?"

"His car..!" Kirti replied the next second.

Das looked at her with surprise.

"The outskirts of the city, you might not have noticed, but it has two ways to reach that place. One is the regular one, from the city, the road where usually no one approaches. Because people know nothing's there. And the other way is through the forest; the road is raw, and no one actually comes there. Cause there's still nothing in that abandoned place!"

Das didn't understand what she was talking about. The detective smiled at him. "And from that raw path, a car drove to the outskirts. There were tire marks from the house to the forest. Isn't the car interesting for us?"

"But we were talking about Nihit." he was getting boggled.

"I'm too, talking about his car! It belongs to Nihit," the detective replied.

"Wait, what?" he couldn't hide his confusion.

"When I visited the site on the outskirts, there were tire marks. Maybe there was rain or something, and I came to know that four cars were there. The car we found at the place belongs to those who died. Two other cars that anyone in the city could drive. But there were tire marks of the Mercedes-Benz CLS." Kirti handed the report to the forensic department. "And that model has only twelve cars in the city. According to the ATM surveillance camera at the other end of the raw path near a town, a car drove to the outskirts half an hour before the three murders you are investigating. That happened to be Nihit's car."

"You don't think Nihit is the one?" the inspector was stunned to hear whatever Kirti was telling him.

"I'm not sure yet. Besides, we don't have anything concrete. But, his girlfriend is dead after half of a month, isn't she?" Kirti replied.

"So, you think there must be a connection..." Das shook his head. "That can't be..." it was difficult for him to digest whatever Kirti was saying. "Alright! What you want to know about him?"

"Everything..! Let's start with his past?"

"He is just an ordinary orphan."

"Still he owns a business." she replied.

"A businessman with millions. Almost all the major cities in the state have his branches of the café. But here is the deal. No hotels, no bars, no discs, no restaurants; only cafés. Nice and a clean business. Nothing's filthy, yet..." Inspector Das added.

"Why is he not in the limelight?"

"Maybe doesn't like to show-off, believes in nice low life things."

"Properties and bank balance?"

"Only enough that he could live a good life and maintain his nice cars. The other car he owns is the usual one, Honda Civic. The rest of his money goes to the orphanages."

"Why not..! He should know how to do it better." Kirti smiled slightly with a mock. "What about last transactions?"

"Clean!" Das replied.

"His routine these days?"

"The last few months, he often drove to Wilson College. He owns the cafeteria there. And attended a few lectures sometimes."

"He attended lectures?"

"For the girl, I guess." Das answered. "And for the time being, depressed maybe; doesn't go anywhere."

"Cell phone records…."

"Most of the calls are of two-three minutes" talks, except with Kayra's number. And that's obvious. Another number that regularly contacted him is Ritvik, which is obvious too. No one from the dead was in his or Ritvik's contact."

Hearing this, Kirti remembered his contact style through letters at the Zero Degree bar and smiled, "Sure! Other people mentioned in the file?"

"He is an orphan; maybe that's why he donates to the orphanages. There are people, though, whom he calls his family; Jay and Gayatri. They are orphans too, and the family is decent. The girl works in the paper mill factory as the head of the operation department, and Jay works with

Nihit, helping him in his business. Their whereabouts have nothing interesting."

Kirti had suspected Nihit, but now she was in a dilemma, what if she was wrong?

"There is another person, his friend, Karan." Das added to his information. "But why would you think Nihit as a suspect, detective? It might be a coincidence!" he said.

"Maybe. The last two murders happened in the wagon; I found the same tire marks." Kirti thought something. "His car was there too, near the abandoned railway tracks. Those tire marks matched the car that drove to the outskirts where you found three dead. The number plate caught on the surveillance camera confirms that it was Nihit's car" She provided another document to inspector Das. "What if these murders are related to Kayra's?"

"Okay, considering your theory, the last two murders of the wagon and the other dead, you can relate to hers. But what about those murders one and a half months back when she was alive?!" inspector Das asked.

"At least, it has something to do with this handsome young businessman! I agree that we don't have anything solid, but it is possible. Besides, he has a nice, reasonable motive for the wagon deaths at least." She smiled, calculating something, and anyone could tell she looked beautiful. "I wouldn't be interested, but there aren't two or three murders. The count is seven, including Kayra."

They didn't count the house which was set on the fire!

The Chase

A car was parked outside the big house a few meters away. The vehicle was hidden enough not to be noticed by anyone. Three people sat inside the car, yawning. They were bored of sitting, smoking, and watching. One of them had even installed the camera on the nearest poles of the building to not to miss anything in any case. But for three days, there was nothing unusual yet.

But this evening, a person appeared in front of them after three days. He wore black trousers and a sky blue shirt, with sleeves folded to his elbow. And the cream-colored frame on his eyes. He was the one they were supposed to spy on. He played with the cigarette in his right hand, didn't light it but threw it, and walked to the garage of his house; there was a sound of the shutter opening. And after a few more minutes or so, there was a sound of the engine start.

The main gate opened, and a car came out slowly. The custom-colored graphite black Mercedes-Benz CLS ran slowly till it met the main road. As soon as it hit the main road, the car sped immediately, almost in a flash.

One of the three remained back while two chased down the black beauty. After chasing the car for about half an hour, the vehicle reached the Eastern area of the city, where the density of houses was less. The car stopped in front of a two-storied building. The young man came out of the car, reached the door, and pressed the bell. Someone opened the door, and once he was in, the door closed immediately.

"What do you think he is here for?" The two sitting in the chasing car talked to each other. The one who drove the vehicle had asked. "For the matter of fact, I don't even know why the heck we're following him." The one sitting in the passenger seat replied. "Should we go inside and check?" the first one asked anxiously. "We should know what's going on inside there. But wait a few more minutes." The other one agreed.

After fifteen minutes, they decided to sneak inside, but again the door opened. The same good-looking person, who had opened the door earlier, was probably two years older than the person who drove Mercedes-Benz CLS, came out and lit the cigarette. He wasn't interested in seeing if someone was following them or what was happening around them. He smoked casually and entered the house in another five minutes.

Another ten minutes passed by, and the person who drove the Mercedes-Benz CLS came out of the house with the same cold look on his face they had noticed since the moment they were following him. The good-looking man also came with him, they sat in the car, and the car sped away in no time.

One of them rushed back to his car, waving something to his partner without even saying a word, and continued his chase. The one who remained back, decided to enter the house.

Dead Already!

The cold wind gathered pace outside the building of the police station. The gushes coming through the window time to time reminded them that winter is in its mid-way only. Inside the dark interrogation room, detective Kirti and a person sat opposite each other.

"Mr. Karan, where were you on 2nd August?" she asked.

"I've given my statement, detective. Is there something wrong?" Karan counter questioned, looked at the face of the lady detective sitting before him, and realized that counter question was quite a mistake. He felt uneasy. "Alright..! I was below the Seminary Hills. A friend of mine came to the town after so long and asked me to come over. I wanted to introduce him to Nihit for a business purpose. I waited for Nihit with my friend, maybe an hour or so, but he didn't appear. Just when I was about to leave the place because his cell was out of reach, I received the call from Jay and reached over Seminary Hills."

"Which friend?" she looked straight into his eyes.

Say it or not, Karan was nervous for the moment, "Sachin Dixit."

"Where were you on 15th November?" her next question was ready as prominent, not to mention she took her profession seriously. Karan maybe didn't know, but three people were murdered that day.

"What's wrong detective? That's not even the day when Kayra was dead," he looked tired, "I don't remember exactly what I was doing that day, but in the evening I was in the town near the forest, say outskirts of the city, to pick up

Kayra."

"What do you mean?" She asked with a curious look.

"Nihit called me to pick her up. He was in a hurry; he came up with something."

"Where did he go? And why do you remember that particular thing and not the whole day?"

"That day, someone tried to kill Gayatri. She was kidnapped that evening. That's why! I learned that fact after I dropped Kayra at her hostel," Karan frowned.

"What?!" Kirti was shocked to hear this. She took her cell out and asked inspector Das to cross-check the department's database about that case.

The detective asked Karan about the incident and he told her whatever he knew. She asked him to wait for some time and left the room. He was helping with the case even though he wasn't involved or it had nothing to do with him.

After half an hour, inspector Das returned with the report. "What do we have?" Kirti asked him as soon as he entered the room. "Nothing!" Das replied, "No complaint registered on her name. Not the same day. Not in a week. And even, till the day, there is no complaint in any police station of the city."

Kirti was even surprised to hear that. "What? Why didn't they?" her thoughts were taking shape, and doubts were getting clear and precise. She returned to the interrogation room and asked about the same to Karan.

"Are you kidding me, detective? Someone tried to kill Gayatri that day! The matter wasn't messy because Nihit had reached on time. If not, she might be dead already!" Karan was confused and shocked, too, to know that they didn't even file a complaint.

"How did he reach on time?" she asked instantly. Her mind had gathered pace already, her eyes not fixing on either object in the room.

"I, I don't know!" Karan replied. "I thought he might have registered the complaint. Why wouldn't he? And if he didn't, perhaps I shouldn't have told you about the incident." Karan said, thinking something, his hands automatically reached his forehead, and he wiped his face. He looked tense.

Kirti looked at him once, thanked him for helping her with the case, and let him go.

When Karan left the station at 6:20 pm, her mobile rang. She picked up the call, and inspector Das could see the changing expression on her face from surprise to shock and then to anger. "Bring him to me, get him here, NOW!" She roared at the other party authoritatively. After she hanged up, inspector Das asked, "What's the matter, detective?"

"They found another two bodies, in the bloodbath, with bullets in between the eyes." Kirti provided the information, "my people were on watch, and the bastard committed the crime under our nose!" She could not hide her anger anymore.

The black beauty had lowered its pace at one of the corners that another white sedan overtook, and it suddenly turned and stopped in the mid-way, blocking the whole road. There were screeching noises of the tires. A person stepped out of the white sedan and pointed the gun at the windshield of the black beauty. "Step out of the car." Nihit stepped out of the car. "I'm arresting you on the charge of two murders!" The person said roughly, showing his badge.

Nihit shook his head slightly and looked at his partner once, his partner nodded, and Nihit frowned, looking at the ground. Nihit co-operated with the cop and sat in the white sedan. The white sedan sped into the city towards the police station, and the traffic was cleared shortly.

The watch was showing 7:10 pm on the wall of the police station. Nihit was once again sitting in the same room. But this time, the person before him was going to be different, which he didn't expect. Or maybe he had expected the same person. There was a camera in the corner and a mic on the table at both ends. In the other room, inspector Das assured everything was alright and waved a thumb to Kirti.

As the lady inspector walked into the interrogation room, Nihit read the tag on her chest. Kirti Desai. 'Damn, why she has the killing intents in her eyes', he thought. It's been a year since they met for the last time. She walked to the chair and sat slowly, her eyes fixed on him. No one would dare to ask her, but if someone asked, she would not admit that she was attracted to this young man sitting before her. With the calm face, long silky hair, and black eyes under the cream-colored frame, there was a charm and an invisible aura around him.

"Why did you kill them?" was the first question she asked. She looked at him with the fire in her beautiful eyes, which probably didn't suit her, according to Nihit.

"I did not kill them!" he denied flatly.

There was no trace of any fear or regret in his voice.

"My men watched you!" she mocked him.

"They watched me going in and coming out. And that doesn't prove anything, I guess."

Kirti rose from her chair and grabbed his collar. "Bastard..!" she mumbled, looking straight into his eyes. He, too, didn't even blink for once. She nothing but has to let go of it for the time being. 'She does lives up to her reputation', Nihit thought, which was true indeed. "Bring the evidence, detective, and I'll co-operate." he said calmly.

"I see... And do you think if I had proof, I'd need your statement or confrontation?"

"See, you don't have it," he frowned.

'Damn! He knew he was on watch', Kirti thought as she heard him.

"Okay, why didn't you register the complaint about your sister, Gayatri?"

Nihit was surprised to hear this question. But he was calm beyond any emotions. "They were dead already! The next day's newspaper had it on the front page. So I dropped the idea to do so."

'This is too much,' Kirti thought. She now was sure that it was him. She could easily hack into his call records or tap his cell, but she avoided it purposely; it would be useless anyway. He had left no proofs, no fingerprints, or any link that could help her. They found no weapon with them, neither in their car. Though she had a theory, that theory was useless without any evidence.

"Can I go now?" Nihit asked, looking at the puzzled face of Kirti. "You cannot keep me here for no good reason. Besides, as you are saying, you don't have any solid proof against me and cannot prove anything."

As soon as he completed his sentence, there was a knock on the door. The good-looking man with him in the evening was back with the lawyer. Kirti could only sigh in frustration while watching the back of Nihit walking out of her sight and the police station.

After he left the police station, she could hear someone blowing a whistle !

A Tired Lover

The custom-colored graphite black Mercedes-Benz CLS stopped around three kilometers away from his house. After the interrogation, Nihit did not go to home. He stepped out of the car, and the good-looking guy smiled wryly. Ritvik had been with him since Nihit was sixteen. He had seen Nihit smiling for the first time when five year angel had entered his life. Today Nihit looked broken and tired to him, that too for the first time.

Nihit walked to the dark alley. There was an eerie silence; one could hear another person's steps. The tree branches allowed the golden light of the streetlights to scatter on the ground. The poles were centered over about 40 meters.

After a decade, Nihit had met Kayra, the love of his life, and someone snatched her away from him. He was in pain. He lit the cigarettes one after another till the box was empty. The eyes under the frame contained moisture. And in the next few moments, he realized the last time he cried was when his mother left. He removed the glass frame from his eyes and strolled on the road putting his left hand in his pocket, thinking nothing, or maybe something. But his mind was not calm. He had made up his mind about where he wanted to go.

He reached the area where he could notice a few people walking here and there. He sat on one of the benches in the lonely place for a long time. After some time, someone patted his shoulder from behind. He looked at the person. It was Kirti.

After her duty hours, she changed into her usual outfits.

She was wearing a loose shirt and a knee-length skirt. She had a sweater too; it was winter. Her hairs were open, they were long, and no one could have noticed it when she was on her duty. He was still in the same outfits, a sky blue shirt, and black trousers. Sleeves still folded; he looked messy.

"What have I done now?" his tone was harsh yet low.

"Nothing!" she replied. "What are you doing here, by the way?"

"Nothing!" he replied and walked away from her to where he had decided to go.

He walked a few steps, and she didn't stop him either. The arrogant one seemed sober now. Suddenly he stopped, turned around, ran a bit, and leaped on her. Kirti fell beside the road, and a biker missed his target. The knife fell beside her. As the bike hit Nihit, there was a loud thud! Nihit flew in the air and collapsed on the ground with a summersault. That caused him an instant pain. The biker had jumped already. He was covering his face with the scarf. The young person seemed fast. He reached out and threw his right leg in the air, landing on Nihit's stomach. The impact of the kick caused enormous pain. He tried to crumple, but another leg blow hit him on the jaw. Nihit spilled the blood through his mouth; his corner of the lip had a cut. Before he could smash another blow, the biker got the kick in his back. Kirti had regained her composure. The young biker turned around.

Kirti waved her left hand on his chest, but it was blocked, and she got a slap on her face and lost her balance. The young biker jumped immediately, and Nihit got another kick on his stomach. "Ah.."

The young biker did not wait longer; he knew Nihit

wasn't easy to kick. However, he acted fast. But once Nihit regained his composure, he would be in danger. Besides, Kirti was there too. Though she was his target tonight, he didn't know how Nihit appeared from nowhere. He started his bike, accelerated immediately; the motorcycle made a big noise, and vanished. There wasn't any point in noticing the number plate. There wasn't any!

Nihit was at his usual composure shortly. He stood up slowly, "Fucking bastard!" He spat out the words with anger. He reached out to help Kirti, offered her a hand, and pulled straight. "You okay? Why did he want to kill you?" He asked, his voice had concern for her.

"I don't know..., it could be anyone holding a grudge on me, cause what I do is just..." She stood up and soothed her sweater and her skirt. "Anyways, he seemed to have more anger on you than me!" She looked at Nihit's broken corner of the lip.

He glanced at her with a hint of surprise, listening to her sentence and looking in the direction the biker vanished.

"Where do you stay? Go home. It's not safe for you now, and get a protection." his tone turned authoritative.

"I'm a cop. I can protect myself." She replied.

"Yeah, I can see that!" He looked at her face once and turned. Kirti's face turned red as she heard his sarcasm. He walked a few steps with difficulty, stopped at a distance, stretched out his body, and left.

At the bar, Zero degree, at the corner table, he sat alone, gulping a whiskey's bitter liquid. A lady walked by, sat opposite him, and ordered rum for herself. Nihit tried to ignore her but couldn't.

"Why are you following me?" he asked her finally.

"Thanks!" Kirti said with a low tone.

"I do not admit what you want me to."

"I know that you won't. Why don't we talk?"

"I don't like to talk much," he replied.

"Alright then. Let's have a drink together."

"I don't invite you." Whatever she tried, he almost rejected everything, but he wasn't rude with his tone. He looked like a drunken person, and he was.

Then he didn't talk until his next drink was finished. "Why do you look like her?" he asked innocently. She looked beautiful, which reminded him of Kayra.

Kirti knew who he was referring to.

"You think so?" she asked with some mischief in her voice.

No one would believe that the lady had interrogated the same person an hour ago, claiming that he was a murderer. And now they were having drinks together and conversing with a hint of romanticism.

Kirti had known him for two years. Though she didn't know anything about him, she only knew him. He was a decent person. Unlike all other people out there, lust lurking in their eyes, he wasn't like them. He was different. She liked him. She met him for the first time at one of the parties in the city. He didn't like parties and crowded places but needed co-operation for his business, so he was there. And Kirti wasn't like any other ordinary girl; she was a well-known, beautiful, intelligent detective. She had clear visions about her ambitions in her life. She thought he was just another guest at the party when they met for the first time

                         The Whistler

as she didn't know him. She fell for him. And a year ago, she even had asked him for a date; he was the first one she had expressed her feelings to. But he had rejected her politely while boys around were dying to talk to her. But after a few more meetings, she learned he runs a business. She didn't know how he started his company but could tell that he was passionate about it.

After that, she met him in the interrogation room almost a year later. She didn't expect to meet him there. The first time she learned about Kayra's death, she was shocked. But there was nothing she could do for him. And further, in the investigation, she found him as a suspect. As with inspector Das, she could not reveal that she knew Nihit, hence pretended she didn't know him. She didn't suspect Nihit anymore. She was sure it was only him and knew the motive behind it. Kayra was his life, and now he seemed lifeless. No one would survive his wrath for snatching his life away. She even could not collect a single piece of evidence against him; hence she knew what he was capable of. With his status and sources, what he can do and cannot! Whatever he does, no one could even put their hands on him if he is not willing to. She could not even imagine what status he had and what kind of skills he possessed. She just knew a little bit about him. Though her hands were already reached his collar, she could not let him commit another crime. He had had enough, and she was there to stop him, even though she knew she would fail. But she could try at least; her duty did not allow him to kill anyone.

She remembered he had never touched the wine before this in any of the parties he attended. She knew he was cold with his nature and behavior, but he did not disrespect her.

As for now, he was acting innocent after getting drunk. Sure enough, the wine was helping him with his emotions. He could still remember the person he loved but could not decide what to recite. And that was making a difference!

"You know, I missed you!" said Kirti, trying to distract him from his pain.

"But I did not!" his eyes were tipsy now.

"You should have!" she fed him the snacks from the plate, and he ate them obediently.

"Why do you still love me?" he looked into her eyes.

"I don't know. But sure, I do." she finished her glass. "Do you have a story to tell?" she asked.

"I don't like stories. I like poems. Poems with rum, whiskey, or either kind of wine in it. Having it in the poem feels like someone splashed it in the air!" he replied.

"You were supposed to tell me a story. I don't remember a poem for you right now." Kirti said, making a sad face.

"But I do. Kayra's eyes had them, and I would read it. They would make me feel tipsy." Nihit smiled, looking at the whiskey in his glass, and Kirti watched him, tilting her head slightly, her right elbow placed on the table and her cheek on her palm.

Nihit lit his cigarette and walked out of the bar at past eleven while he put his other hand in his pocket. The waiter or manager or anyone didn't ask him about the bill. Kirti waved a pointer to the waiter for the bill. But the waiter said the manager told him not to provoke this person. The owner told the manager that this person would never visit, but if he did, do not provoke him, whatever be the circumstances.

She wasn't surprised to know that, as she knew who

the person was she was having drinks with. She didn't think much about it and walked out of the bar. She didn't know that the owner was Shirish Ahuja, the CEO of ARK textiles. This was his one of the businesses, and he owed his life till death to Nihit.

Outside the bar, Nihit stood leaning his back against the tree and smoking. Kirti reached him, took the cigarette, and threw it. He didn't say anything. She slowly weighed herself on him, and her hands went around his neck.

"What are you trying to do?" He asked in a hoarse. He wasn't in the state to resist. "What do you think I am doing?" she whispered, and his left hand reached around her waist. Her lips slowly reached to his. They kissed. They kissed passionately. Both were so fierce that she started biting his lips, and her lips bled in the play. He sucked the blood passionately, and she accompanied him. She didn't mind melting down. It had begun, and there was no going back.

In the morning, he opened his eyes as the sun's rays bothered him. The place looked unfamiliar. The lovely decorated room, no messy things; all things seemed to be placed appropriately with neatness. He glanced around the room and tried to rise from the bed, realizing that someone's hand covered his chest.

He could see her half face, her hair covered the other half, and they were messy. But she looked sweet. Her outfits were untouched. She still was in her loose shirt and the knee-length skirt she was wearing the last night. He looked at himself once and realized that nothing had happened.

Nihit was drunk, and it was his first time too, to drink. But she was sober when she approached him to kiss. She drank enough not to get high; she wanted to accompany him. Once it had begun, he could have gave in easily. He was not in his senses. But she was. She could not break the protocols, taking advantage of his loneliness. She loved him.

She brought him to her house and helped him to reach her bed. He passed out in less than a minute. She was about to leave the room, but he grabbed her wrist; he was unconscious, mumbling, "Don't go!" She sat beside him, smiling, and eventually, she too fell asleep.

Nihit smiled briskly and walked out of bed. He went to the washroom, washed his face, and went to the kitchen. He made a tea the way he liked with extra ginger in it. When he was making tea in the kitchen, Kirti woke up and realized something. She ran to the washroom and returned shortly. She reached the hall and could hear some noises from the kitchen.

Nihit walked out of the kitchen with two cups in his hands. "Morning!" he said and handed her a cup. She sat on the sofa quietly. The two didn't talk, but there were glances and the sound of sipping the tea. When they were finished, Nihit said, "Okay. I'll leave now," and stood up to leave.

When he was at the door, he heard the voice from behind. "Nihit, you don't have to do this."

"I did not start this," He turned his face slightly, "and if you can trust me, I did not want any of this. The heck with whoever it is. He dragged me into this. He has to pay whoever he is. He has to die! I'll make sure he dies, with my bare hands!" and left the house.

Kirti could only sigh helplessly.

The Crime

Kirti had just arrived at the station and called out for her subordinate. Now that she knew why people were getting murdered and who was behind all this, she was relaxed. As she knew Nihit wouldn't go out randomly killing anyone. Eventually, she has to close the case with no evidence because her theory could not prove the fact. Nihit wasn't going to leave any proof for her, which she had figured out already as he could commit the crime under her nose while her people chased him.

But now she was thinking about why and who would want to kill Kayra.

The subordinate came with the file in his left hand and the bandage on his right.

"Where were you, and what happened to your hand?" she asked.

"One of them is still out there, hiding somewhere. I got the news from our sources," The subordinate provided information, "and this happened in the conflict while I tried to catch him."

"Ma'am, we still have a lead on him. Right now, he is moving towards the outskirts of the city." The subordinate told further.

Vizag - the city of destiny to be called had a nice view that day. The sea on his right looked stormy, same as him, while he drove the car. He throttled the car to full of its capacity. This wasn't the first time Nihit went like a crazy person. The black beauty ran recklessly to the outskirts of the city. His mind wasn't at peace since he had lost it long ago. He thought something and again stomped the accelerator pedal, shifting the gear to its top.

After riding for half an hour, he reached the city's outskirts, the other side of the Seminary Hills. As Nihit stepped out of the car, he saw a handsome-looking guy sitting on the rock, smoking. A person lay in front of him unconscious, and his hands were tied. Nihit took the bottle of water, sat on his legs, and poured it on the face of the lying person on the ground.

As the water touched his face, there was a movement. Before he could open his eyes, Nihit kicked him in the stomach, and the person groaned in pain. His face turned pale when he was fully awake, realizing his hands were tied. He stood up, struggling.

Nihit walked to his back and untied him; kicked on his left leg; the goon knelt on the ground. He was scared to open his mouth, even to scream. He knew his fate after learning what had happened to his companions.

"Don't let your mind allow even to think that you can escape." Ritvik said, playing with a gun in his other hand.

When the subordinate provided the information, Kirti rushed to the vehicle. "Come on, let's go." She ordered, and the aid followed her suit. In less than twenty minutes, the vehicle reached out of the city.

"The last GPS location is the Seminary Hill's other side. I wonder what he is doing there. That place is just plain ground with some rocks in between. People don't usually go there. Even gangsters avoid the place. There is nothing to hide." As the subordinate provided information, she glanced at him once. She realized something, and the speed of the vehicle increased drastically. The subordinate was puzzled by her behavior.

"He didn't go there. Someone has taken him!" She told him, avoiding Nihit's name.

The subordinate looked at her once and looked forward through the windshield glass, trying to recollect the order of things that happened. Who might it be? The last time someone was on watch. Nihit! Holy shit! And he got the chills all over his body as he remembered the conditions in which bodies were found. The day was in the middle, and the sun was on the head. A police car ran wildly on the road.

As Nihit faced the goon, a few sweat drops gathered on his forehead. He knew his fate, but he could not just let someone kill him; he had to fight back for his life. He punched Nihit's face with his right hand, but Nihit blocked the attack with his left hand, grabbed it tightly, and slammed his right elbow on it; a sound of breaking something reached his ear. And the goon screamed terribly. He knelt immediately, holding his broken arm with another, still crying loudly. Suddenly he felt a pain in his chest, he looked at it, and his chest had a cut and the blood-colored his shirt red. The agony drove him wild; his screams turned into wails. Nihit threw the knife into the valley, made a move, and his knee landed on the goon's chest; he collapsed back with a loud thud and lost consciousness. As the goon reached the soil, Nihit noticed a police car heading towards them from a distance.

"Tie his hands and cover his mouth," Nihit said, looking at Ritvik. He followed the instructions and did the same as asked.

A few minutes later, a car reached to them. Nihit untied

his hands, and Ritvik took out the handkerchief covering the goon's mouth. As soon as Kirti stepped out of the car, she yelled, "What the hell is going on here?"

"Nothing, detective; we were passing by. I thought to stroll over here. You know, I like quiet places. And we found him in this state." Nihit gestured at the unconscious goon.

The subordinate reached out, and Ritvik helped to bring the goon into their car.

"Clever!" Kirti appreciated the lie. "But don't worry, once he is in his senses, we'll know how you found him here." Kirti gave him a stern look and said, "Don't leave the town. As for now, you can go." And she returned to her subordinate, talked something, and they returned. Nihit and Ritvik waited till the police car was out of their sight.

"Finish him inside!" Nihit said as soon as the car vanished.

"But..." Ritvik wanted to say something.

"He is guilty. Kill him!" Nihit said and walked to the driver's seat of his car.

"Once the goon is awake, he will accept his crime of killing Kayra with his companions. For now, Kayra's case would be close. For the wagon deaths and other murders, this goon could be a witness against Nihit. So both the cases are solved." The subordinate said while they were driving towards the hospital.

A Waiting Girl

After Kayra recovered from the accident, instead of dropping her at the hostel, Nihit took her to his house.

Gayatri opened the door and was stunned to see a girl with Nihit. She pretended to think something and said, "So finally, my cold brother let someone into his heart!" and winked at Nihit. He was embarrassed, scratched the back of his head, and introduced Kayra and Gayatri to each other. Gayatri welcomed Kayra into the house. She was happy for her brother, who was finally in love. She was always afraid of his cold attitude and was worried if he could accept any girl in his life.

While sipping the tea, Gayatri inquired about the bandage on Kayra's forehead and asked her how did they meet and all that stuff. "You know what, I'm glad you could break that ice wall," Gayatri said excitedly. "Last time, almost a year ago, a girl proposed to him, and he rejected her, saying he belonged to someone else. The girl was a detective, and boys could die for her beauty. But here's my cold brother!" Gayatri made her eyes big, blinked a few times, looked at Kayra's face, and asked, "Wait, is that you? But you said you met a couple of months ago only." Kayra's face turned red, realizing he hadn't let anyone near him all these years. But she didn't answer Gayatri. Kayra and Gayatri became lovely friends in a short time.

Nihit was in his study room thinking something. He had sensed the threat, which was a warning to him. Both incidents with Gayatri and Kayra could not be just a coincidence. Jay walked into his room and watched Nihit playing with the cigarette he hadn't lightened it. Nihit noticed Jay but didn't say anything. Jay asked Nihit watching his worried face. "What's wrong with you?"

"What happened to me?" Nihit counter questioned casually.

"What are you thinking of? You look tensed." said Jay. Nihit nodded but didn't say anything.

The next day, Nihit dropped Kayra at the hostel and told her he would be out of town for a few days. She didn't say it, but she wanted him with her, to spend her time with him; after all these years, he was back to her, and she didn't want him to go away. She had met him after so many years, and now she wasn't willing to be apart from him anymore.

Two days later, his cell was out of reach. A week later, she found his cell switched off. Kayra contacted Gayatri and got the same news that his cell was off. But neither Kayra asked Gayatri about his whereabouts nor Gayatri mentioned it. Ten days later, his cell was on, but someone else picked it, telling her that he was in the middle of something. But he didn't call her back. Kayra was angry. How could he not call her even for a minute? Is he swamped this much? What the hell was he doing day and night?! Did the person who received the call even tell him about her or not? The next day she scolded the person who picked it up. It was Ritvik. She ordered him to tell Nihit that she wanted to meet him and would be waiting for Nihit at their regular place in the evening, and if he did not show up, she would be there only and would not move an inch till he arrives.

The following night she waited at their regular spot. The evening was getting darker, and it soon turned into night.

The road was empty. The night was getting colder and colder. She was wearing his favorite outfit and a sweater over it. There was no sign of anyone. He didn't arrive.

She called him at about eleven in the night. Again, Ritvik picked up the call and told her to return to the hostel. She threw her cell on the road in frustration, breaking it into pieces. Her eyes contained moisture. She knelt on the ground and covered her face with her palms. She cried and cried. But he did not arrive.

At a distance, in the dark, a car was parked. Because of its black color, it was unnoticed by everyone from the evening. Nihit stood leaning back to his car, watching Kayra throw her cell and cry. He, too, threw his cigarette. He wanted to go, but he did not!

The next day she caught a cold. As soon as the sun rose from the Eastern horizon, she took a cab to Nihit's house. Gayatri opened the door and watched Kayra trembling in anger, "Where is he?" Kayra asked despite knowing that he was not in the city.

"What happened, Kayra?" Gayatri touched her hand and immediately took it back. "What the hell! Where were you to get this cold? Come." Kayra resisted but did not let her go and dragged her to the sofa. "Sit here and do not move, silly girl!" Gayatri ordered her. It was her caring nature.

Gayatri took her cell, dialed the Doctor's number, and asked him to come over. "Nihit will be back soon. He went somewhere in the evening yesterday." she told Kayra to calm down.

"He is in the town?" Kayra was fuming in anger.

Gayatri was puzzled by the question, thought for a

second, and realized something, "I'll get a tea for you." and rushed into the kitchen. As Gayatri returned with a cup of tea, she watched Nihit entering the house. She put a cup on the table in front of Kayra, glanced at her brother once, looked at Kayra, and said, "I'll leave first." and escaped into her room.

As Nihit saw Kayra sitting on the sofa, he walked towards her and stood in front of her. "I'm listening, explain." Kayra said, looking at him with fire in her eyes. But he didn't answer. She waited for him to answer, but still, he did not. Finally, she stood and wanted to leave, but he grabbed her wrist. Kayra rescued her wrist with a jerk. "You don't want to hurt me always, like this, do you?" The broken words came out of her mouth.

Nihit had expected at least a slap, but she didn't. She loved him. Tears rolled down through her red eyes. "I'll just walk away if you want me to. Why do you have to do all this?" She looked messy. His hand reached out to hers, but she retreated again. "What do you think of yourself?" she was much angrier than she was expressing in her words. And much more scared than ever to lose him, again!

Nihit pulled her into his embrace, but she did not resist this time. She clung to him, hugging him tighter, her tears making his shirt wet on his chest. He rubbed her head while his other hand reached to her waist. All her anger vented into the air. He lifted her face holding her chin, and wiped her eyes. He looked into her eyes and didn't say anything, and she grabbed him again.

After another fifteen minutes, the doctor arrived. Gayatri too came out of her room. After taking the medicines, Kayra was better than in the morning. Nihit sat near her head while she was asleep.

After that day, Kayra lived with her new family. She was happy; she had a lovely family.

A month or so passed quickly. And one day, she was bored sitting in the house and doing nothing. In the evening hour when Nihit returned home, Kayra wasn't there. He was about to call Kayra, but the screen flashed, showing her name. She asked him to reach Seminary Hills, saying that Karan had planned something for him.

And that's when Nihit got a threatening call. After that call, he called Jay to reach the place explaining the situation only in a few words. Today he was at the café near the Seminary Hills.

As Nihit reached the place, he saw Kayra sitting on the bench at a distance. There was a crowd of people roaming around. There were stalls for food and many things, and people enjoyed their time with their loved ones. Kayra looked at Nihit and rose to walk toward him, making a way through a crowd, but she knelt on the ground suddenly in the midway. She felt pain and agony on her neck. Further, her eyes became blurred. She heard Nihit screaming, approaching and grabbing her, not letting her collapse back on the ground. She tried to speak, her lips trembled, but couldn't speak, her shirt became red, and she slowly closed her eyes.

People gathered around, murmuring what was happening there and asking each other why the beautiful girl was lying on the ground while a young man was holding her in his arms. He was crying, and his shirt, too, was getting red.

A figure stood unnoticed by everyone at a distance but observed everything with cold eyes, putting his left hand in his pocket, while another hand played with a cigarette. As he crushed the filter, He turned and left while blowing the whistle.

After cops took Kayra's body, Jay was afraid to talk with Nihit, he was late. Nihit was late too. Anyone could notice the coldness in the eyes under the frame. His face had turned pale. One could see only rage and the fire that could burn anyone. He felt the pain, the loss, the defeat. And the rage!

A Comeback

Nihit was already an introvert, and after what happened, he was devastated. He wasn't in the state to do anything. Now he scared everyone who dared to look into his eyes. He wouldn't sleep much. He would wake up at midnight with fear in his eyes and sweat on his forehead. As for Gayatri's knowledge, something else was also haunting him other than Kayra. A name, Lily. Gayatri was bothered about the name Lily. But she could do anything about it; and Nihit wouldn't talk about it either. Jay had to take over the business for the time being, along with Ritvik.

The cops looked good for nothing. That's why he didn't talk about the threat. Besides, his sources were relatively more substantial than that of the police department. There were always shadows to protect his loved ones in his absence. That's how he could stop the harm to his sister, Gayatri. The police would be unable to reach the killer as his own sources were at loss for the time being. The case was out of their hand. The murderer didn't leave a clue. Or, in case there were any, the department was too dumb to notice it, until the lady detective, Kirti, interfered.

Someone had committed two murders, and that's what had Kirti's attention. After another fifteen days or so, there was another murder. The murders were brutal that made the deaths miserable. Both the scenes were no less thatn horror! When the cops reached, they immediately sealed the area so no one could enter the site. The journalists and reporters were prohibited even from looking at the bodies of the dead.

After months, when he realized that he couldn't sleep

in peace, he had to do something. Now that Nihit had money, power, and the sources, he asked Ritvik to spread some words with his contacts, and in less than a week, they found that a group had taken a contract to kill Kayra. The sources confirmed the girl's picture and the people who were involved. There were six men. Nihit wanted all of them at once, but only two were together in the city. It didn't matter anyway; they were going to tell where the rest of them were! Once they fell into the robbery trap, Ritvik played his next move; arranged for an advocate and another person to provide the envelopes. Now that someone had bailed them, and the same person wanted to offer a big deal, the goons didn't consider reaching the abandoned railway track in the south. Besides, places like that were perfect for handling any agreement. They were right. This was the ideal place to handle the deal!

Nihit wasn't involved in anything until the last moment when he killed the goons. The goons faced the good-looking man and a person of twenty-five. The handsome man seemed older than a year or so than Nihit. Without wasting much time, Nihit held the mobile in his hand, showing Kayra's picture and asked if they knew her. Their faces turned a pale watching picture of the girl.

"Who the hell you think you are? You with the police or what?" one of them asked arrogantly.

"Just speak whatever you know, and it will be easy!" The good-looking man said with disdain in his voice.

"Well, you think you'll ask us something, and we'll tell you that much easier, plus you try to threaten us!" the goon laughed.

"No! I didn't think you would co-operate." Suddenly, Nihit swung his right hand, and it landed on his jaw. The one who spoke had got that slap causing agony on his cheek.

The good-looking guy lifted his leg and landed on another goon's chest. The goon collapsed back, and the weak metal sheet of the wagon made the noise. The goons were shocked to watch turn the two men hostile all of a sudden. The first one pointed his gun at Nihit. The goon didn't notice, but the good-looking guy had made a move making that gun-holding goon buckle on his knees. His grip over the gun loosened, and it fell to the floor. Suddenly, Nihit's knee smashed the mouth of the same goon against the wall of the wagon, and he spilled the blood on the wall. His teeth pierced into his tongue, and he screamed terribly.

The other goon, who had got only a single foot till now, had enough time and took out his knife. He pointed it at Nihit and stabbed, but Nihit dodged it. He grabbed the hand holding a knife, turned the wrist around, and the pain made that goon lose the knife. Nihit bent, picked up the blade, and stood straight with a jerk, and the goon had an extended deep cut on his stomach. The blood squirted everywhere; with another stab, Nihit entered the knife into the goon's left arm. That scream he made could tear the eardrums.

Both Ritvik and Nihit dealt with them alternatively. Ritvik had broken the arm of the first goon he was dealing with. The goon lay on the ground, Ritvik put his shoe on his palm, and his right leg moved; the first move landed on the chest and another on his jaw. He gifted him a few more kicks in his stomach.

Before breaking their bones and splashing more blood, Nihit asked a few questions. Vijay, their leader, had got the contract to kill the girl. Before they got killed, Nihit got everything they wanted to know.

After their companions were dead, the others were alert. But that didn't matter. In another fifteen days, the third guy was down. Next month while Nihit was on the watch, he didn't come out of his house. He wasn't even interested in going anywhere either. Once Ritvik made the arrangement of soundproof things in the place and snatched two goons, Ritvik conveyed his message to Nihit through Jay. The two had a no different fate. The punches, kicks, broken bones and ribs, the unbearable pain, wild screams, and the bloodbath. Under the nose of the cops!

While the last one was hiding from his death, he also was on the list of cops. When Kirti's subordinate found him, he escaped. The cop fell on the gutters edge, hurting his right hand. But to his unfortunate, Ritvik's people had an eye on him too. Ritvik was unaware that the goon had his cell on when he took him to the outskirts of the city. And just before the goon was about to die, Kirti reached on the spot!

A Shadow

All the deaths had a common link between them. Kayra! Kirti had solved why and who had killed the goons. But Kayra's murderer was still out there. She couldn't think of a reason why someone would kill Kayra. Everything she could think of led her to the dead end again. If someone wanted Kayra dead, she was!

However, the bloodbath had begun after Kayra's death only! Kirti was doubtful if she was on the right track. Is it related to Kayra's death, or someone else was the target? Was it only killing her, or did someone have an alternate motive? And if someone had an alternate reason, what could it be?

Kirti had visited the location where Gayatri was taken after her kidnapping and the town near the forest area, where she had found the surveillance camera of the ATM and suspected that Nihit was behind those murders. And eventually, she was sure that it was him. But Kirti had not visited the Seminary Hills, where Kayra was murdered. Kirti called inspector Das and asked him to come over. While driving with him to the Seminary Hills, she recited the report of Kayra's murder. Das narrated whatever he had. No person to be suspected with the possible motive to kill Kayra, no murder weapon, nothing. Except he had found an old Fiat, and someone seemed to use it. But that too couldn't help him.

When Kirti and inspector Das reached the site, he told her where and what they found in their investigation. Even Kirti checked the car just to get nothing. She looked around and found something that made her smile.

She looked at inspector Das and asked if he had visited

the place she was looking at.

"Yes. We asked people around there, too, if anyone noticed something unusual or something that could get their attention, but that was useless too." Das replied while both walked to the café around 40 or 50 meters.

"You checked that?" Kirti asked him, gesturing at another surveillance camera on the opposite building of the café.

"No." Das looked at her face.

The café owner had purposely installed it on the opposite building to get a broad view of the café. Das asked the owner for the footage of the particular day, holding his badge in front of his face. There was a chance the murderer reached a few hours before. That was obvious.

The video started, at 3:35 pm a person walked in casual outfits approaching the old Fiat. He had a cap. He stood there for a minute, looking in the crowd's direction, and sat in the car. Then there was no movement till the next one and a half hours. At exactly 5:10 pm, the same person stepped out of the vehicle showing his back to the camera. He still wore the cap and had his head down all the time. He slowly walked into the crowd; at a distance, something slipped through his sleeve to his hand. He walked and eloped into the crowd. And then there were people rushing and gathering around someone.

They re-played the recording from 5:10 pm onwards just to get nothing. A person was wearing the cap, with a knife and a watch on his wrist. They could only watch his back. For the fraction of moment, someone could notice his face when he stepped out of the car. But, he wore a cap and kept his head down. Plus, the camera was focused on the café, and the distance was too far to notice anything clearly; plus, the quality of the video made it difficult to recognize the face. Kirti was even more frustrated not to see his face. It looks like he was aware of the camera.

"What is the matter, detective? Someone else also asked for the same footage in the noon. Usually, we don't give it, but I thought it had nothing interesting, plus the girl offered a nice sum of money, so I gave it to her." The owner said.

Kirti was puzzled hearing about the girl, but she remembered, also the anonymous Intel was given by a girl when her all the sources had failed. Who might be the girl? Kirti had utterly forgotten about it. She could ask about it to Nihit. As stated by the owner, there was nothing useful. But maybe, the person who wanted the footage knew it could be helpful. As for the fact, cops couldn't see if there was anything. But there was something. There was!

Late in the evening, Kirti got the news from her subordinate, who was on a watch at the hospital. The goon was in his senses. She slipped her cell into her pocket and rushed toward the hospital. Kirti was relieved that she had finally stopped Nihit from committing another crime. But she was concerned that he would be in danger if the goon became the witness against Nihit.

She reached the hospital and watched the goon still groaning in pain. As Kirti sat, the goon thanked her for saving his life from the monster he was still horrified of.

"He did this to you, right?" Kirti held Nihit's photograph before the goon.

As soon as his eyes fell on the photo, his eyes widened, and his face changed suddenly. He felt it was difficult to breathe; sweat gathered on his forehead, "Y..yes!"

"So, you are ready to give a testimony against him?"

"No!" the goon retreated in a second; "I don't want to die!" he was unaware of the fact that he was a walking dead man, already.

"Easy." Kirti tried to calm his fear. "Why did you kill Kayra?" she asked further.

"I did not. I did not kill her. Neither any of us did." The goon refused to take the charge. "Before we could act, someone else had her. We were happy that someone did our job and we still had the money. If we wanted to do it, we wouldn't do it in broad daylight while so many people roaming around." he took a pause and said, "someone framed us to death."

"Who?" Her questions were straight to the point.

"I don't know; we just received an order from our boss, with the photo, money, and the note which said what we had to do." The goon replied.

"That's it?" she wanted more out of him but could not get it.

He had nothing.

"Ma'am, you trust him?" the subordinate asked with hesitation after they walked out.

"He just returned to his life from death. He wouldn't be lying. Take him into custody and record his statement." She left the hospital and headed to her house; it was late already.

Early in the morning, at the hour of four, her cell rang wildly, and she awoke with sleepy eyes. But the moment she heard the other party's words, her sleep was long gone. "Damn it!" she slammed her palm on the table.

The goon was dead inside the jail!

On His Sleeve

Kirti watched the video clip where a man with the cap steps out of the car and walks into the crowd. She didn't recognize it yet, but she was sure that there was something at least, and she was missing it all the time. Her guts were bothering her that she couldn't figure it out.

After watching the tape almost twenty times, Kirti was about to give up on the video, but something clicked into her mind. She replayed the video again, and went through the last minute when something slipped into the killer's hand, a blade. She paused the video, and her eyes widened, forming her mouth into a big "O". "Holy crap..." The words came through her mouth.

"Madam, apki chai..." Ravi, the sixteen-year-old, said, placing the tea on her table.

After what the last goon had told Nihit, he couldn't bear it anymore. Vijay and his companions didn't kill Kayra. Since Vijay was also murdered by someone, nobody had any clues about who had brought the contract to them. Karan sat along with Nihit at his house. There was a silence. The silence was broken when Nihit's cell rang. It was Ritvik.

"Does this name mean anything to you, Sachin Dixit?" When Nihit heard that name, his expression changed, and his face darkened. "He is responsible for the attacks on Gayatri and Kayra. For sure, he is the one who killed Kayra. I have the footage of the Seminary Hills. Some girl, Akriti, had sent it in your name. I didn't find anything, but you should go through it; maybe you can find something." and the call was disconnected. Karan and Nihit found nothing other than a person walking out of the old Fiat, covering his face with a cap.

Nihit slammed the laptop to close. Gayatri ran out of the kitchen after hearing the loud sound but didn't say anything when noticed Nihit. Jay too came out of his room and said nothing.

But something clicked in his mind, and Nihit hurriedly opened the laptop again. And there he had, he had something. As he saw a man with the cap stepping out of the car, his eyes narrowed, and his heart started throbbing rapidly. When his eyes fell on the hand with a blade, Nihit noticed something.

Everything related to the person wearing that thing started to gather in Nihit's mind. Jay probably didn't ask him to come over the place; how did he reach there? He was there... Neither did Nihit tell him; instead, he had asked him a favor. How the hell does he know?

His mind ran recklessly, his eyes turning red and gloomy. When Kayra had an accident, no one knew about it. Not even Jay; when he brought Kayra to the house, that's when Gayatri and Jay learned about it. But how did he know? He was there at the hospital... Nihit's face was redder with anger, and his heart was pounding unevenly.

The watch! Here was the clue for him. The watch on the sleeve reminded him of a person, and his face turned dark. His eyes became colder than ever. It ended just a few days later when Nihit told him someone was spying. He took a few days to create an alibi and let Nihit think he was digging about the spy.

Nihit didn't doubt him or cross-check because he was the one to do mostly that kind of things for Nihit. He was sneaking around and finding things about people. When Kirti asked Nihit about Gayatri, she mentioned that someone wanted to kill Gayatri. How could Kirti say that someone wanted to kill Gayatri? Gayatri was kidnapped. Only Nihit and Ritvik knew that the goons had an initial plan to kill her. Because they had extracted the crucial details they wanted, before killing the goons. How did Kirti know about Gayatri's incident anyway? And then Nihit recited Kayra's last text; Karan had planned something for you... And Nihit realized now what he had planned...

"Did you ask anyone to come over when Gayatri was kidnapped?" Nihit asked Jay in an authoritative tone.

"No!" Jay glanced at Nihit, "what happened?"

"Then how and why was he there?" Nihit roared anxiously.

"Who?" asked Jay.

In the time Nihit talked to Jay, he had played his card. There he was, just before them, standing five feet away. Suddenly he moved, reached out, and grabbed Gayatri, and she was at gunpoint in less than five seconds. Gayatri trembled in the fear, "W., what are you doing, Karan?"

At this moment, Kirti opened the house door and was stunned to witness the scene before her eyes. Her hand reached for her gun, but a crisp voice fell on her ears.

"Watch out, detective! Have you lost it?! There is already someone at the gunpoint! I thought you would care for her!" Karan said playfully. He looked at Kirti and said, "Detective, why don't you take your gun away? I'd appreciate that. However, you seem to have no other choice!"

Kirti was clever enough to notice the watch on his

sleeve in the videotape; it's just that she took more time. She remembered Karan wearing the same watch, in his second interrogation and headed directly to Nihit's house. She didn't want to alert him by calling or doing anything. But when she reached, it was late. Now that she had no option, Kirti put her gun on the floor and pushed it away with her leg.

After a momentary silence, Karan said, "now that you know who I am, it's better to play it straight." Nihit didn't reply to that. The voice continued, "You know, I've waited long enough! To snatch everything that belongs to you!" he moved slowly towards the chair where Nihit sat, switching the gun to his left hand. Jay froze where he was; shocked to know the mastermind behind all this, the person whom he called his friend.

"You shouldn't be here!" Nihit glared at him.

"I admit that I shouldn't be here!" he said with disdain in his voice; his right hand swung into the air and landed on Nihit's face. And there was a crisp, loud sound as Nihit stood before him. But the slap didn't affect Nihit much. "Well, eventually, I will kill you too! As for the time being, I have a gift for you!" said Karan.

Suddenly he turned his left hand, shot Nihit in the right leg, and Nihit knelt on the floor, clasping. The next move wasn't expected, his right leg hit Jay's chest, and he fell back to the ground. The other gunshot hit the floor near Kirti's feet, breaking the floor tiles and blocking her; the dust powder flew in the air.

There were three more gunshots. Another two hit the glass wall, making a big sound of glass breaking and shattering towards the floor. Everyone tried to cover themselves with their hands. The broken wall made it an open area to escape, Karan jumped out of it. Kirti wanted to follow him, but all they could hear was the screeching noise of the tires. And he was gone!

Nihit looked at Gayatri and soon realized where the first shot had hit out of three. She was holding her belly, her hands colored in red. Nihit crumpled on the ground and climbed to her, Gayatri was on her knees. She had pain in her eyes. "Brother...," a few drops rolled down through her eyes. A few more minutes, and she closed her eyes slowly and slept in peace in her brother's arms.

Nihit called out her name a few times and screamed. Soon his screams turned into hauling and eventually in wails! Jay there fell numb and blacked out.

There is an old saying, trust people but verify! And Nihit had made an exception for this person. How could he? This was a mistake he could not afford. Although, Nihit had trust issues and would verify the details of every person he hired and worked with, but he made an exception for Karan and did not cross-check anything. He was always there, helping Nihit, and gaining his trust.

He wasn't Karan. It was a cover. His real name was Sachin Dixit. The chapter of Nihit's life that no one knew about!

The Roots

The time being sensitive, Nihit needed his parent's attention. But they couldn't offer their love for him regardless it was affordable. While he craved for his parent's love and affection, things were getting ugly between them day by day. A fourteen-year shouldn't have watched his parents fighting daily. That still would be fine, but Nihit watched them fight to the peak that they were on the verge of getting divorced. And in the next few months, they did. His parents certainly loved him, but they couldn't show it to him for a reason. One should be adequately nurtured at that age, but he was unfortunate.

He wouldn't talk much and became silent. Won't say what he wants, what he feels, or even what he thinks.

He made friends with a group of five boys. They weren't his age; while he was fourteen, four were almost eighteen. But like his parents, they wouldn't ignore him. Though he would not say much, they still noticed him.

One of them was Sachin Dixit. Sachin was a simple boy. He was the only one of Nihit's age, and because Sachin was in this group, Nihit made them friends. Finding your exact mirror personality is difficult, but to Nihit's fortune, he met Sachin. There were many things they would have their independent perspectives on, but they respected each other's point of views. Their understanding was remarkable. Apart from Kayra, Sachin was someone with whom Nihit could be seen quite happy. Sachin would occasionally be in the group, and so would Nihit. They didn't hang out all the time with the group.

Sachin would take Nihit to his house sometimes. He lived with his mother, father, and a beautiful girl Lily. She was an adopted child. Sachin's parents dotted her with love, just as they would have if it were their daughter. Though, Nihit didn't see her a single time and wasn't even interested to see her. But Sachin would always talk about her, and that's how Nihit knew she was beautiful. Whenever Nihit visited Sachin's house, Lily was out somewhere.

Although Sachin's parents dotted her like their daughter, he had different feelings for her. And with time, Lily, too, reciprocated with the same feelings towards Sachin. They were in love. When Sachin talked about Lily, anyone could tell he was in love. Nihit just listened to everything Sachin talked about Lily, his plans with her in the future, and all that stuff.

Everything was good, but one day, things happened, and everything changed. That day, the death's diary added a few deaths that were going to happen almost after a decade!

The group Nihit and Sachin were friends with wasn't worth it. Till they realized, it was late for them both. Things happened which made their lives miserable.

One day while the so-called group of his friends was sitting at their regular place when Nihit reached, they were talking about a girl passing by. Nihit turned, and well, the girl was charming. Sachin wasn't there. As Nihit went to them, their discussion almost died about the girl. But one of them asked, "What do you think of her?"

"Her? Well, she is pretty!" Nihit smiled.

"I need a favor," the same guy said.

"What kind of favor?"

"Would you ask her to meet me, I have something to talk about, and it's necessary." The guy pushed his luck.

Nihit glanced at him; for the time being, there was nothing to get suspicious about looking at his face. Nihit glanced at them, and they nodded, "She knows him, don't worry. He wants to talk to her; besides, you'll be there." That made Nihit assured that there wasn't anything fishy.

"Why would she listen to me? We even don't know each other!" said Nihit.

"Tell her Sachin's name and bring her to the abandoned house of the town." And he left. After some time, others also left.

Nihit waited till the girl returned from the direction where she went on her bicycle. When she arrived, he approached and tried to convince her to come over with him, even though he was a less talker and kind of an introvert. The shyness which reflected in his behavior didn't even let the girl think twice about anything that could probably go wrong with her. However, Nihit didn't feel it right when he walked with her out of the town. Because if they know each other, and the boy wanted to talk to her, why use Sachin's name?

Nihit asked her name while walking, and now he knew who she was. Lily! That was making sense why Sachin's name worked. She was the girl Sachin talked about all the time. No wonder Sachin appraised her too much. She wasn't less. He wanted to take her back at this point, but they were already infront of the abandoned house.

The house had no roof over it. There were only half-broken walls. Usually, no one would come over here because there were rumors about the place being haunted. And just at the back of the house, the forest begins, a kind of scary place.

In the afternoon, time of about 4 o'clock, both entered the house of walls and saw the four sitting over one of the half-broken wall, waiting for them. "What all of you doing here?" It was the first question from Nihit the moment he saw them. For the time being, he was sure that something, not something, everything was wrong!

"He said he wanted to talk to her! Not all of you." Nihit pointed at one of the boys and looked a bit hostile.

He looked all of them in their eyes, and noticed lust lurked in them. The same eyes he had seen before, but now, they seemed deceptive. Those he called friends, behind the mask of friendship were heinous animals, not even humans. But he figured it out late.

Nihit looked at Lily and told her to leave immediately. But one of them jumped at the door, blocking her way out. "Let her go." Nihit roared, but that didn't change anything. Instead, they burst into laughter. As for Lily, she was trapped. She knew exactly that they wanted to harm her dignity, and she was scared as hell. The guy in front of her grabbed her wrist. Nihit knew he wasn't any match for them; they were four, elder, and stronger than him.

Nihit bent, lifted a brick and smashed it on the boy's head. His grip on Lily loosened, and she tried to escape, but another one blocked her. The boy, who had his head broken, grabbed Nihit, twisted his fists to his back, blocking his every action. "Son of a bitch, you'll stop us. You think you can?" The boy spat out.

Lily screamed for help, but no one was there to hear her screams. The boy threw her back on the ground. She begged for the mercy. "Let her go, bastard!" Nihit yelled again. The boy, who was holding, released him, slapped hard that Nihit lost his balance, fell to the ground, and blacked out.

One of them leaped on her and tried to shut her mouth; she gave a strong bite and got a slap in return. Another one grabbed her both hands, and the third one pressed her legs, making her struggle useless. She resisted, she cried, but there was no way out. The stream of tears flew through her eyes. One of them reached out and tore her sleeve to the shoulder and blocked her mouth with that torn piece of the sleeve. She wanted to scream but could not. She struggled to stop him. But her struggles failed. A hand reached out to her chest to rip out her clothes. She closed her eyes instantly, she wanted to die before whatever was going to happen. But they would not even let her die. She was still resisting, but nothing could stop whatever was happening...

But at the last moment, out of nowhere, they heard footsteps, someone humming and approaching the house. The group looked at each other and ran, leaving the girl in a half-ripped state. Nihit, too, regained his composure, pounced on the scarf, ran to Lily, and covered her. He, too, had to run; if not, he was in danger. He glanced at her, he wanted to apologize, but there was no time. "Go home," he said, and he too vanished shortly.

But the next day in the evening, he was shocked to hear that Lily had committed suicide by drinking a poison. The group had made the fuss of nothing defaming her. Lily was humiliated by everyone around her, which made her mind drive to commit a suicide.

Sachin was out of the town that day with his father. Everything happened in his absence. If he were there, he wouldn't let happen anything of it. He and his father reached only to watch the crowd outside their house. When his father heard of Lily's death, he fell sick, fainted, and fell unconscious, never to wake up, and died on the spot of a heart attack. He dotted Lily with more love than his son. Watching his father not move, Sachin collapsed to the ground.

When he opened his eyes, Sachin was in his bed. He slowly walked out; his mother told him everything what had happened the day before. He walked to his father and Lily. He called out for his father, but he didn't reply. He called him out even loudly, shaking his body but still there wasn't any reply. He walked to Lily, sat near her head, and took her into his arms. "You, you cannot break your promise!" Sachin caressed her hair, "you said you wouldn't leave me! Look, even father is not talking to me. Only you can convince him to talk." he sat there for hours, holding her in his embrace.

Sachin was broken. His world had fallen apart, and now, his mind was filled with the rage. He wanted all of them dead who dared to touch Lily. He wanted all of them dead who had hurt Lily, and that caused his father's death. He could not spare them. They were monsters to do such a heinous act. They didn't deserve to live. They must die for what they have done. They must. They have to. Whoever was involved had chosen their fate themselves. There is no other way in between and no other choice!

He had arranged the gun from local goons. The goons didn't mind selling a firearm to a fourteen-year-old boy because people usually sent boys to buy that stuff to avoid getting caught. However, Sachin plotted the alibis and sneaked out and completed the job. He killed all the four boys the next day itself, at the same place, in the abandoned house.

After killing the four, now it was the time for Nihit. According to the four, Nihit was responsible for what happened to Lily and his father. They blamed Nihit for everything, telling Sachin it was Nihit's idea. In a hope that Sachin will spare them. But he did not!

Sachin could confront Nihit before killing him, but now that nothing was going to change, he wasn't even interested to look at his face. It had happened already, and nothing was going to change the fact that his father and beloved Lily were no more in this world. No person lies before their death, so the four must be talking truth, Sachin thought. But they were not; they hoped that after telling that Nihit was the mastermind, Sachin would spare them, but they were wrong. The next target was Nihit!

On the third day after Lily's death, in the evening, when Sachin saw Nihit and his mother in the market, he found a way to do his job. He reached out and sat in the car parked at the end of the market. To Nihit's unfortunate, the key was in the car. Sachin didn't know how to drive a car, but who cares? He just wanted to crush them; what he knew of driving was enough for him. But when he did it, his mother pushed Nihit aside, and the car ran wildly after hitting her. Police closed the case in the name of just another hit and run case, but there was the only person who knew that it was not!

After burying his mother, Nihit left the town the same night. There was nothing left in the city. The town had given him too much pain. He had lost his mother. And he could not face Sachin after the tragedy, unaware that only Sachin was the one who killed his mother.

After whatever happened, Nihit could not sleep well for almost a decade. He lost it. Nearly every night, there was a nightmare. He would be awake in the middle of the night, sweating. There was regret! That occupied his whole life. The only face that haunted him was Lily! He never thought his past could destroy him to the ground, into ashes!

After that, Sachin chased Nihit like his shadow, everywhere. There were obstacles, there was a time he would be desperate to kill Nihit, and even he had chances, but he did not lose himself, he waited. After learning that Nihit has something to lose, Sachin decided to snatch it first that Nihit should know the pain of losing.

When Nihit was in the wind and Sachin could not trace him, he approached Jay and became a friend. When he approached to Jay, he could not use his original name, so he played along with the fake name and gained his trust. When the time arrived, Jay introduced Sachin to Nihit. He could not reveal his real identity, but when it was the time, he would. One of the obstacles in his path was Kirti. Her investigation could have ended Nihit in jail. But Sachin didn't want that. He needed Nihit outside. Nihit was destined to watch himself getting destroyed. Sachin himself wanted to punish him. He even tried to kill Kirti, but out of nowhere, Nihit appeared, and he missed his target.

After some more failures, he finally achieved what he had wanted his entire life!

Epilogue

On the outskirts of the city, a white Fiat slowed down its pace after almost running wildly for an hour near the windmills. Till Kirti could try to stop him with the forces of her department, he was long gone. The car stopped at the street tea stall; a person stepped out and ordered the tea and a cigarette. All his life, all these years, he waited to destroy Nihit's world. And now that he had succeeded, he was happy from the core of his heart. All this time, he had to chase Nihit. But now, for his final target, he did not have to track or follow him. Nihit himself will come to him. That's what will lead him to complete his revenge!

After completing the tea and a cigarette, he walked back to his car, blowing a whistle!

* * *

After a week, Nihit visited three most important ladies of his life in the evening past five and came out of the cemetery. The black Mercedes-Benz CLS reached the orphanage named Future.

He sat on one of the benches out of the house and waited for someone. A few minutes later, someone tugged his sleeve and asked him, "What happened to your leg?" The innocence in the five-year-old girl's voice was overloaded. She had watched Nihit walking difficulty.

The same angel visited his café with her parents. He found her in the orphanage when he visited there for some supplies of fruits and other necessary stuff. And he learned that her parents died in the accident.

"Nothing, love! How are you doing here?"

"You know, I miss you. Mother said you love me. But you do not come here to meet me for a long time." she complained.

Nihit noticed a shadow near him. It was Kirti. But she didn't say anything to him, and neither did he. Nihit lifted the girl in his arms. The girl reached out to his pocket for the chocolate, and Nihit had it. Like old times.

"I missed you too!" he said truthfully. He did. "Love, I'll come soon to meet you again. But now I have some work outside of the town, okay..."

"No. When you go, I miss you, don't go!"

"I'll be back soon, love!" he stroked her head gently.

The little angel blinked and nodded in affirmation.

While Nihit was playing with this angel, his cell chimed, showing a name - Akriti.

Kirti casually picked up the call as she didn't want to disturb Nihit. The voice fell on her ears, "Would you care to meet me?" The voice was familiar to Kirti. She remembered the anonymous intel. That's when Nihit returned, and she handed over his mobile to him.

Nihit was leaving the orphanage while talking over the phone, and Kirti watched his figure getting blurred and disappear. Kirti looked at the child and thought she had to visit this kid in between as Nihit wasn't going to be there.

Kirti was wondering about the girl who had helped to trace the criminal and a voice she had just heard moments ago over Nihit's cell. She also remembered some girl had taken the footage from the cafe of Seminary Hills. For the matter of fact, Kirti knew what Nihit was going to do now.

When she was also about to leave, Kirti's mobile rang, and she answered the call, "Detective, we have a situation." The voice of the other person had terror in it. "Twelve bodies have been found at Zero Degree bar into pieces; it looks like someone sliced them by the blade ! ! We have sealed the area; please come here fast..."

Kirti was shocked to hear the news. She looked at the direction in disbelief, terrified..., from where she could listen to a roar of the car engine, in which Nihit had left...

This time, death's diary was forced add a lot of chaos in it, loosing the count of deaths...